BIG TIME

by

ROYSTON ELLIS

KICKS BOOKS
NEW YORK, NEW YORK

Books by Royston Ellis
published by Kicks Books

GONE MAN SQUARED
Collected beat poems, 1959-1967

BIG TIME
The autobiography of an pseudonymous pop
star in Britain's Swinging Sixties

THE FLESH GAME
Beach boys in Las Palmas in the 1960s
live by the rules of the flesh game.

RUSH AT THE END
A respectable city clerk falls for a young
student in this tale of forbidden gay love
in London suburbs in the 1960s.

SWEET EBONY
Four women in search of romance discover
more than they expect in Kenya in the 1970s

THE MALDIVES ADVENTURE
A swashbuckling historical yarn
by a master storyteller about the
Maldivian hero who saved the islands
from Portuguese colonization
in the 16th century

Cover model: Howie Pyro

An expurgated version of this fictitious
autobiography of a pseudonymous British pop star
was originally published in England in 1964 with
the title *Myself For Fame*. The language of the period has
been preserved for authenticity; the names of the
pop star and characters appearing in this story have
been changed, to protect the bad, the bent,
the beautiful and the blameless.

BIG TIME

Easy, easy,
    break me in easy,

Sure I'm big time,
    cock-sure and brash,
But easy, easy,
break me in easy.

Sure they've been others,
    I know the way,
But easy, easy
break me in easy.

Let me hide,
    warm deep and wet.
Under the blanket
and between your thighs

And easy, easy,
Aaaah—break me in easy.

From: *Gone Man Squared* by Royston Ellis
published by Kicks Books, USA, 2013

INTRODUCTION

I'm a bastard. Not in the literal sense, as it happens, but in the slang sense, which is far worse. I'm perverted, deceitful, vicious, immature, narcissistic, gonorrhoeal, depraved, unprincipled, dissolute, and a slag. I'm also a teenage idol.

I've read some of those smarmy biographies by other stars saying how lovely they think they are. They might as well give the books away free to members of their fan clubs, the amount of truth they contain. All right, I know stars daren't tell everything for fear of what it might do to them. But that doesn't worry me; you see, I have got nothing left to lose now.

I've been there and back. Climbed to the big time, got shafted and fell apart.

The pop business is a very eccentric set-up. The values are all wrong for a start—they must be for a boy like me to earn a £1,000 a week just for having a good-looking face and a passable voice. The exaggerated importance of being a singer would affect the most level headed character. It did me. My only consolation is that I'm not alone, although I cracked. There's no one in the pop world who's not tainted by some perversion or craving which he first turned to for relief from show business pressures, and then through a definite desire.

You name me any of today's teenage idols and I'll tell you his kink. With one of them it's gambling, with another it's his mother; one likes schoolgirls, and one enjoys being whipped by his manager (really!); one's got a big death wish, another a fixation for negresses; one likes boys and another likes drugs, one's crazy for leather, and one's... well, the list is endless. And me?

It's my kinks which have laid me out now in this Harley Street nursing home suffering from, as the press politely call it, "nervous exhaustion." I've been here five days now, doped up to the eyes; with only a wardrobe and a TV set as my audience, I've had plenty of time for thinking.

Looking back, I suppose it isn't surprising that I should finish up like this, but who would have guessed it at the beginning? I've not always been the person I am now. Just look at this cutting from the profile feature of the top peoples' paper *The Sunday Guardian*. This came out in August, 1961.

"TEENAGE IDOL"

"At a time when the world hovers over yet another crisis, teenagers are remarkably unperturbed by events. They are concentrating on the things which have always appealed to them: sex, clothes, and records. Instead, if anything, they are buying more records at this particular moment than at any other time this year. This is mostly because of a young man called Danny Gabriel who has sold nearly a million copies of his first disc released in April.

"The life expectancy of a teenage idol is something which as yet no sociologist has cared to estimate. There are idols who, after an initial period of hit discs, sacrifice their popularity with teenagers to consolidate their talents in other fields. On the other hand, there are singers who slip from the charts and, however much they try, fail to regain their popularity in any direction whatsoever.

"Now, teenagers are campaigning for yet another new idol: Danny Gabriel. They are flocking in thousands to join his fan club; they mob him mercilessly wherever he goes; they break into near riots at his shows; photographs of him are being sold at a premium and anything which bears his name, mark, or the slightest suggestion of being owned or even touched by him, is being snapped up and jealously treasured.

"The phenomenal success of this boy (a success which has astonished the most optimistic of popdom's chiefs) prompts one to ask just how long can it last? But if this is a question which worries Danny Gabriel, he does not show it.

"Known as the 'Singing Angel', in appearance, Danny looks younger than his nineteen years. He is a slight boy, 5ft. 4 ins. and eight stone. He wears his blond straight hair very long accentuating the striking bone structure of his face. His eyes, set wide apart a Grecian nose, are brown. It is his eyes, peering under dark brows, which one first notices about Gabriel as he takes in every detail of a person before glancing modestly away. He looks far too innocent to be alive.

"His home is in the Cheshire village of Thickley where he was born and bred. He is very much a product of community life, going first to Sunday school when he was six, then graduating to the church choir, the youth club, and the Scouts, leaving school at fifteen to work on a farm. He kept that job for three years before deciding to come to London at the beginning of last year in search of fame and fortune. It was only five months ago that his dream began to come true.

"He is a dedicated boy. His sole interest in life is music, his music. He spends hours each day with his guitar, playing and singing to himself. He probably even sleeps with it, for his devotion to music is so great that he has absolutely no sex, nor social, life at all. His exclusive attitude to life cuts him off from everything. He is completely unaware and unaffected by the impact he has on his fans.

"He is a quiet boy whose simple economy of speech has frustrated many journalists eager for a sensational quote. Ask him how much money he earns and he will give a puzzled smile and shrug his shoulders. Ask him what he had for breakfast and he won't be able to remember. Ask him what his interests are and he'll point to his guitar.

"But on stage, this seemingly inarticulate artless child transforms into an athletic creature capable of whipping up more excitement than a cup final. From the moment the curtain rises on the seraphic figure standing in the centre of the stage, a non-stop shriek of ecstasy grips his audience. He sings, shouts, writhes, and stirs up an unbelievable frenzy without ever once making a vulgar wriggle or any movement which would offend the vicar of his church back home in Thickley.

"If teenagers must have idols, they have chosen very well with Danny Gabriel. He is still a countryman at heart, and has a countryman's wholesome sincerity. Any unhealthiness in the rigid intensity with which he regards his music can easily be cancelled out by the fantastic purity of his personality. He is an idol worth respecting and one whom a long life-expectancy could be a good thing for fans as well as for him."

Well, get that! Fantastic, isn't it, how people can be conned. That's how I was a couple of years ago; at least, that's how journalists thought I was. But even then I was living a lie. So what went wrong? How did the "innocent idol worth respecting" become the sod I am today? It all began when I gave myself for fame and reached for the big time.

DANNY GABRIEL,
Spring, 1964.

CHAPTER 1

It was a world of darkness and strange clockwork-like fantasies, maybe men strutting around the village pump or a clown doing a mechanical handstand outside the Queen's Arms. There was a boy there, running jerkily in his loose fitting grey shorts down Thickley Lane. He was six years old, and trying to fly. He took off abruptly like a puppet and was never seen again. A great hand plunged down and scooped out a lump of cheese which sizzled in a pan somewhere in that world of darkness. It surprised me.

The air was damp; a drift of dew from Gunn's Meadow swept over the church and into the main street. The vapour settled slightly on the village. Mrs. Hughes's dog, let out as she took her six o'clock walk to the privy, sniffed his way along the gutter. High on the hill behind the Post Office, cows were grazing placidly on the Manor Estate.

The vague figures in my waking-up mind were changing as consciousness gradually filtered through. A boy kicked a ball high into the air; it came down near me. I raced for it, dodging Jones from the Welsh team. A sharp-angled kick and it was in the net, straight by Williams still hovering over the other side of the goal. I had played a good game . . . On your marks, get set, go; and I did—tearing down the long stretch of one hundred yards to the English master at the tape holding a stop watch. The crowds, Mums and Dads in Hopwich and it wasn't even market day, shouted. I burst my lungs in a flash eating up the yards, watching those flying elbows of Douthewaite and then hurling myself at the already broken tape to finish second. I had run a good race.

The cock chortled, niggling me awake. I knew it was time to get up, but just one more minute, perhaps. I turned, feeling the snug caress of my pyjamas as they twisted with the sheets. One blanket only had been warm enough. I tried to blink open my eyes, rubbing them impotently with a lazy fist. Surely dawn was creeping into the room, the first shafts of sun, itself still hidden, streaking across the sky. It was time to get up and call in the cows for milking, but I couldn't move.

The cock's crow suddenly became a shriek—thousands and thousands of screams vomited over me, violating the air round my bed with a suffocating smell of sweating naked women. A blood vessel behind my ear started pounding guitar music, driving the insane beat of a rock tune through my mind. The shrieks grew louder, each strident feminine voice desperately calling for me. They were selfish screams and I was scared. I tried to run, but the bedclothes were pinning me down. Someone was tapping a drum solo on my head; the smell was choking me; the screams were deafening. I was being beaten, choked, and knifed to death. I died.

Looking down from a great height—like seeing the world in a cinema from the film projectionist's box—I saw a young man on stage. About twenty-six, I suppose, singing to a theatre-full of anticipating women and their intrigued escorts. Occasionally, a shout would break the surface-concentration of the audience as they watched this man move slowly over the stage, crooning expertly into his hand-held microphone. The backing group, more used to rock numbers, struggled with his ballads. A true professional singer with a small reputation, he was holding the audience well as they trembled for the star.

They clapped him when he finished, and prepared to laugh at the compere bouncing on with a sick joke. Then, with the tabs closing behind him, they realized that they were on the verge of the big moment. They drowned the compere's attempts to entertain them, taking up a chant throughout the theatre. They bellowed a name in unison, conducted by the compere who'd abandoned the struggle to introduce the star. All he wanted was for the nits on stage to set their instruments up so he could piss off.

The audience's chorus rolling down on him like thunder, he peeped behind the tabs, pleading with the boys to get things ready. Drums set up, drummer in position. Two guitarists in black suits, one in white. All there, all set. The compere grimaced with blasé exasperation (to overcome his inferiority complex) and turned to shout back at the audience.

"Here he is, ladies and gentlemen," ("*You stupid humpers*", he was thinking). "The star of our show . . ." Thunder blocked his words; the lights faded; the tabs opened and there—picked out by a white spotlight—was a boy with a guitar.

The screaming rose to a crescendo and then, as the audience became aware that there He was, standing before them, looking, just looking, it tailed off. The boy, like a pale ghost with his blond hair and white suit, stood in front of them, guitar strapped across his chest, and raised both his hands, outstretched like a prophet. The audience stirred in sudden silence.

His hands came down slowly, the right one arching round to the centre of his guitar, the left one turning back and gripping the neck. His eyes, focused on some celestial object in the circle, slowly came to life with an expression of sheer joy. His whole face seemed to give out with youthful happiness. In a quavering voice he ejaculated a tiny shout of rousing contentment, and then it all happened. There was a crash of drums, the stage lit up revealing two guitar-playing acolytes and a drummer, and the rocking began.

The slight blond creature on stage certainly knew his job, or enjoyed his music. The wild raving sound he generated filled the auditorium and gripped each one of his listeners with a private thrill. They responded either to his music or to him—hearing his sound as the noise which had revolutionised pop music—or seeing him as an untouchable but definitely desirable being from another sphere.

After twanging and raving his way through his act, the curtains dropped, cutting his public abruptly off from the image they loved. He tore off his guitar with shrieks for more still in his ears. He ran down steps to his dressing room, dodging through pests who, on some official pretext, always seemed to be lurking in the wings to grab and baffle him with inane chatter.

Pushing open his dressing-room door, he made straight

for the armchair. His manager leapt up quickly, and the singer slumped in it, crashing his guitar down on the mirror-walled bench. He reached for the open coke bottle, sufficiently laced with unseen whisky, and drank deeply. In that gulp and draft he tried to shut his ears to the screaming which followed him from the stage and now engulfed him, seeping through the slammed door and window.

He watched his manager run hot water into the, sink, carefully laying his towel, soap and flannel out for him.

"There's a bloke from the local paper to see in a minute, and a photographer. I've screened them. And there's a fellow says he knew you at school; wants to bring his bird in. Name of . . ."

The manager's voice droned on and the screams took their proper place as background noise like overhead aircraft or busy traffic, as the singer rose up to prepare for the normal duties of fame.

◆ ◆ ◆ ◆ ◆

Coming back to consciousness, I could see me there, bustling around changing; commenting on the birds, wondering about the act, saying a few words to journalists, looking sweet for the waitress who brought my supper, signing autographs for usherettes, raving about a record, reading the musical papers; behaving normally as I did every night of my show business career. I was oblivious to those screams, my name chorused until it merged into an indistinguishable background chant.

Oblivious, that is, until my dream, my nightmare, pushed me back to the living in this bed. The dreams have been going on for days, wracking my sick body with the continual horror that was surprisingly my life. Pressure seeping out of my system as I lie in bed, this bed, always this bed.

I don't have to open my eyes to see the lime green blankets, the little bedside table with the telephone they won't allow me to use yet, and those terrible pots of hyacinths balanced on a tray on stilts at my feet. The only comfort I can cling to at the moment is that cool hand someone has just laid on my forehead. There's the soothing voice of Ireland being friendly and assertive. She's all right. The dark haired one they call Mary. Mary. *Christ! Where am I?* Still here in this lousy cure-hutch!

"It was the screams this time," I try to explain, fully awake now propped up on my pillows. I don't mention the smell of women—I am disappointed that the two dozen naked lovelies I had sniffed draped around my bed aren't here. I could hump a few now. *Christ! I haven't had sex for a week*. It'll drop off.

"Sure, and you'll be having a few more dreams, my pet," croons Mary, "but don't let it get you down. You're a grand lad and this'll soon be over."

She must be joking.

"Take this pill now, and you'll feel better."

Bleeding liar! She knows it's to send me to sleep again.

♦ ♦ ♦ ♦ ♦

When you're ill, stretched out on your back not feeling energetic enough to read, too lazy even to get up for a piss, thoughts go tumbling through your mind. When you're ill like I am, it's doubly worse. I just couldn't keep the thoughts and memories out of my head at the beginning. That's why they drugged me up, I suppose. And to keep me from wanting a drink. Sex, drink, and pop music have laid me here, prostrate in bed—my favourite position!—but without any of the comforts to make it worthwhile.

Have you noticed how sick people always have a distinctive smell about them? Smells have been meaning a lot to me lately; they're my secret communication with the outside world. I can smell something, even remember a smell, and they don't know anything about it. Of course, I'm entitled to keep things from them. I mean, I'm paying for it all so I ought to decide what I want to tell them.

I can smell a bit of Spring at the moment, even here in Harley Street. It's not like Spring at home, of course. The rich smell of the middens, of fresh milk as I pummelled it from cows, the awakening countryside, flowers popping up everywhere, lambs being born, all that jazz. I guess I miss Thickley at the moment.

Thickley is a quiet compact village about fifteen miles south of Chester, well sheltered from the main trunk roads. About five hundred people live there and each one of them is well aware of what the other 499 are doing, thinking, and even dreaming. The peace and exclusiveness is rarely shattered. Twice a day, at eight in the morning and five at night, a battered single-decked green bus rumbles up to the church. That is the Hopwich Special and the only link with the outside world for those without cars. Hopwich is six miles away. There is a school there, a railway station, a cinema and, on Wednesdays and Saturdays, a market.

For those who don't have to go into Hopwich, or Chester, for work, there is not much excuse to leave Thickley. Life there is well organised. There are three shops. The main one is the Post Office which sells everything from toothbrushes to tomatoes. That's my parents' place. There is also a butcher's and, surprisingly, a dress shop. Delivery vans of various kinds call frequently throughout the week as well. That's the place I lived in for eighteen years.

My world then was a cluster of houses and terraced cottages grouped round the intersection of three roads, to Wales, Chester and Hopwich. A smaller road, Thickley Lane, cuts into these alongside the church. The church dominates the whole village, towering above the pump and horse trough on the grass triangle formed by the intersecting roads. Life revolves round the church and the Queen's Arms opposite.

That pill the nurse gave me is beginning to work. It's hard to concentrate but I want to give you a picture of the kind of background I come from. It's all down to my mother, really. She was an outsider in that village; I'm sure it's something to do with her own questing spirit that I never stayed in Thickley as I should have done. Mum turned up in Thickley from London one Saturday in the middle of 1938.

She was a small, dark-haired virgin with an air of determination about her when she got off the market bus and paused under the church, letting the farmers jostle her as they made for the Queen's Arms.

She surveyed the evening scene with obvious pleasure, a relish which lit up her whole face. She nursed her suitcase happily, not noticing the curious stares the farmers and village folk were giving her. On the bus she had been the main point of murmured discussion, the passengers wondering which village she would get off at. It surprised the folk of Thickley when she alighted at their doorstep, for they didn't know that anyone was expecting a visitor.

When I was a kid, I never tired of hearing mum tell me how she must have stood for five minutes, taking in everything about the village. She noticed its neatness and, as the bus chugged off up the road to Chester, the relaxing peace which filled the air. She knew she had found the place she wanted. With brisk steps, a much less tense expression on her face now, she crossed the main road. She wondered at first about going into the Queen's Arms, but decided instead to pop into the quaint shop a few yards further on.

She pushed open the door, the spring bell jangling at her entrance. Inside she discovered a new world. There was a restful calm about the store. The shelves, stacked high with musty-smelling provisions, were like a buffer to all the strains she had ever known. There was a pleasant smell of, of what? New cheese? Fresh milk? The countryside! She sighed contentedly to herself, reassured now that the friends, and her mother, who had said she was silly to bury herself away in the countryside instead of going to Clacton or Southend for her holiday, were very much mistaken.

A man, about ten years older than herself, came through the door behind the counter. He limped slightly. It may have been the magic of the shop or her own smugness at having done something she had always dreamt of, or just fate. Alice didn't know. All she knew then was that standing before her was the most handsome man she had ever seen. He had brown twinkling eyes and long sandy hair growing right down his cheeks in Edwardian style sideboards. He looked so strong and healthy.

"What can I do for you, miss?" asked Dad, puzzled by this new face in his shop. She wasn't a country person at all, had a definite air of the town about her. It struck him as funny how a girl brought up in a town looked so much different from a country lass. She looked smart, the perfect little lady, completely unobtainable for the likes of him.

"I've come here on holiday," said Alice, "and I wondered if you know where I could stay."

Their courtship astounded the village. The villagers watched every move from the moment Alice got off the bus until Jack led her up the aisle at St. George's nearly a year later.

I turned up, perhaps because war-time contraceptives weren't all they should have been, on January 23rd, 1942. Dad was down in the shop with a few of his cronies. The village women were grouped in the street outside. A baby, especially Jack Glover's baby, was a notable event. Anyway, it helped take your mind off war. The midwife from Hopwich was there, and later the doctor turned up to see that everything was okay. It was of course, and dad was wild with delight. After being assured that he could do nothing by hanging around, and after being ordered to by mum, he went along to the Queen's Arms for a very rare drink. But not before he had popped into the church and given a little prayer of thanks.

So this was the world I was born into. Goodness knows what powers took my mother to Jack Glover's shop, but a child could never have had two better parents than mine. Ours was the happiest family and stayed that way . . . until I loused it up three years ago. On the whole, I suppose I was closest to my mother. Certainly it was she who devoted all her time to me during the first few years. Dad was often out of the shop, helping people who hadn't got a man about the house because of the war. Mum used to sit me on the counter of the shop, and I'd gurgle happily in my cot while the village mums peered and prodded me. How I used to play up to that first audience!

My parents, as were most people in the village, were regular churchgoers. As soon as I was old enough, they took me along to the Sunday School held at the same time as the morning service. I enjoyed that, learning about the little Jesus. He seemed to be the sort of person I would have liked to meet. I often imagined what it would be like if ever he came on the bus from Hopwich.

We had a little school in the village where all us kids used to go. I wasn't sure about school at first, because I'd have less time to roam the fields and explore. But I didn't protest much and was glad I didn't when I discovered how much use I could make of the things they taught me. Dad used to make me feel very proud when he got me to help him with the shop accounts. I don't suppose I was much help, but I seemed to make him happy.

Since I was an only child, my parents watched every stage of my growing up with almost too much interest. But they were well-balanced parents and never spoilt me. They seldom scolded me either, but then I never gave them much opportunity, for I never did anything really dreadful. Some of the village kids were a bit wild but my upbringing kept me out of that.

I got to like school a lot, and used to study as much as I could. It was a shame that I never seemed to get very far though. I just wasn't gifted with that much intelligence. I used to join in everything enthusiastically, then run home at night to tell mum and dad what I'd been doing. The neighbours, seeing me race home through the village, my long hair fluttering in the breeze, used me as an example to their own children of how a "good boy" should behave. They were all proud of me for some reason, but the other kids never held it against me. I mean, they didn't pick on me as you'd expect them to. They seemed to like me just as much. I was certainly a good-looking boy and had lots of admirers, especially girls. Even before I was eleven there were always one or two girls waiting outside the shop for me.

Girls ! *Christ, how I love them!* I'm sure that there is nothing in the world so enjoyable as a woman. A woman, snug by me now, a woman I can grasp in my sleep, caught up in a dream, tense, hold her close, dousing her with drowsy kisses. A woman, drowsy, women, girls, vague memories; the smell of sun-toughened hay, the aroma of a young girl's hair ... "I remember the first time, long long ago." *What was her name?* What was it?

♦ ♦ ♦ ♦ ♦

A boy in shorts came out of the shop after Sunday lunch. He was going to lie down in Gunn's Meadow and dream. He loved dreaming. Sally must have been waiting, for she came up the road after him.

"Hello, wait for me," she shouted. "Where you going?"

"I'm going to the meadow," he told her. "To lie in the sun."

"I know a much better place to go," she said. "It's quieter there and no one can see what you're doing." She shot a glance at him. "You could even sunbathe with nothing on!"

Two children walked down Thickley Lane to the old barn at the end of Gunn's Meadow. Coming to the high hedge that concealed it from the road, they climbed over the gate. The sun was streaming down onto a small patch of grass just at the back of the barn, away from the road. It was very private. The boy sat down on the grass and pulled off his shirt. He rolled it up for a pillow and sat back contentedly.

"Aren't you going to take all your clothes off?" said the girl slowly. "I think I am."

The boy was too lazy to argue. He just wanted to sleep. He closed his eyes, his thoughts gently drifting off in pleasant young-boy dreams. The girl, sitting beside him, tickled his stomach daringly, watching his face, waiting.

The boy twitched awake, and glanced in mild surprise at the girl somehow naked beside him. He noticed her breasts were small and unformed, but vaguely exciting.

She said his name softly. "My sister told me how to make babies."

The boy didn't speak.

"It's very easy," she went on. "You just put your thing in mine. Shall we try—come on, let's try."

The boy was jerked into a blind panic. Sally's hand had crept up the leg of his shorts and was groping about. He sat up quickly, pulling himself away from her. He saw she'd got nothing on at all; her body was pinkish with little tiny hairs at the top of her thighs. He didn't know what to do. He was sure what she had suggested was wrong. He wanted to get up and run away.

Suddenly Sally was on him, pressing her shaking chest against his. For a moment he tensed to push her off, but relaxed as he felt her soft warm skin brushing against him. It was nice. Her hand was fiddling with his shorts again, and at the same time she was breathing into his ear making it tingle.

"You do it like this, Danny. It's all right. It's lovely. My sister told me, she knows. Come on, Danny, there's nothing to worry about."

He felt her hand slide right up the leg of his shorts. Terrified, he jumped up, grabbed his shirt, and ran off. He ran round the other side of the barn and was just about to dash up road when he saw someone coming. The only thing for it was to go back to Sally.

She was lying flat out on her tummy, her head buried in her hands. Her body shook as she sobbed quietly to herself.

"Don't cry, Sally," he said, kneeling down beside her. It was obvious that her tears were a lot worse than his terror at doing something dirty. "Don't cry."

She looked at him tearfully. "It shouldn't have been like that," she blurted out. "My sister dared me to do it, that's all. She told me what to do, and then she dared me to do it with you."

◆ ◆ ◆ ◆ ◆

My mind flickered as I came round, that incident from the past vividly searing through me. And suddenly I'm thinking of the sea. The first time I saw it. It was at a scout camp in

Wales, the first morning we arrived. I could hear this great noise, like a tractor stuck in a field, but going on all the time.

There was a clump of trees straight ahead of me and the noise was coming from beyond them. I went through the trees cautiously, wondering what I would find. Through the branches I glimpsed a vast expanse of light grey, something like the sky, but not.

Then I was at the edge of the wood and standing high on a cliff. Below me was the sea, *the sea!* I was amazed. I had never dreamt that the sea was so strong and big. Great waves were crashing into the rocks, sending up waterfalls of white foam. I stood for ages, just watching the sea, trying to understand. I knew from school that there were more things to life than my parents, friends and Thickley. But here was a world so big and powerful that no one had dared to tell me. I had found out for myself.

Big deal! I'm sweating.

If only they'd let me have a drink.

CHAPTER 2

There's a guitar over by the window. It's a straightforward Spanish model given me by my fan club—no gadgets and wires. Sometimes when I've been on stage I've looked upon myself as the essential part of a machine needed to produce my music. I felt like machinery, not a person. I just plugged in, strummed the accepted chords, and was away. That's wrong: there's got to be more even to pop music than that. I've always loved the guitar though, and only during the last few months found the whole thing a mechanical, automatic drag. The love of music—my wild zestful style —first came to me during my school days. That was when I'd left the village school at Thickley and used to go to Hopwich each day. If I hadn't developed that love for music, I would have been unbearable.

Most boys seem to get bawdier and more rowdy as they grow up, filling their minds with grand ideas and adult ways, I was the exact opposite. The more I learned about life, the less I seemed to accept. There didn't seem any point, and certainly no glamour, in creeping into the bogs at break for a drag of someone's cigarette. The smut the older boys poured into my ears didn't interest me at all. The nagging and the jokes the others played on the staff and new kids left me cold. I didn't even try to skip school at all. I was in that strange affable frame of mind which for me meant school was something to attend for a prescribed period of time. I was prepared to do that and live within the rules.

I was an energetic kid and hated hanging around. When my dad bought me a bike, it didn't take me long to realise that I could help with the morning milking on the farm. I used to get up at six, cycle along to the farm and milk the cows until just gone eight. Then I went back to Mum's for breakfast before cycling off to school. In the evenings I was back helping on the farm, at Scouts, choir rehearsal, or staying at school for basketball practice. I mention this to show what my early life meant. I was like most kids without any care in the world, but because of my upbringing, I just didn't want to idle my young life away.

In 1955, it happened. I think it was during a geography lesson. The teacher had been called away somewhere and we had been left to study by ourselves. You can guess the row that had broken out in the classroom. The boy next to me, Cavell, I think his name was, was singing. He was going frantic, shouting something like "One o'clock, two o'clock, three o'clock, rock".

I was fascinated, and when he told me that he'd heard the song in a film showing at the Odeon, I decided to go along. The film was a little epic called "Blackboard Jungle" about the American equivalent of us hick-town school kids. It was an "X" film, and even today I still don't know how I got in. Why, I barely looked my fourteen years, let alone sixteen, the minimum age for admission. I know I felt quite bad about it for a time, but it was obviously destiny that I should see the film.

I'm a firm believer in destiny and fate. It's only looking back now that I can see where fate has worked in my past. Everything fits into a terrifying pattern. I'm just wondering what I'm destined for now—flat out on my arse with an un-available nurse and three doctors ogling me.

It was in that film that I first heard rock-n-roll—I didn't know at the time that this was going to have such effect on my life. But that night, as I cycled home, I just couldn't shake off this picture of American youngsters bopping in their classrooms to a background of a reedy voice and honking saxophone exhorting them to *"Rock!"*. It was a squawking catchy beat with a new excitement I hadn't noticed in any-thing before. I remember thinking that if that was what was going on in America, why wasn't it happening here. But maybe it was, how was I to know cooped up in Thickley?

I kept my eye open for another sign of the teenage revolu-tion and patronised the Hopwich Odeon whenever I thought there was a film which might solve something for me. That's how I came to see "Rebel Without A Cause" in 1956. This was a James Dean film about adolescent misfits. I suppose Dean was the first of the teenage idols, someone teenagers could really identify themselves with. I didn't think much of the story as it seemed to be grossly exaggerated. I just couldn't grasp how anybody could behave like that, get himself so tangled up. But I listened to the older boys at school raving about Dean.

In a way, I was a bit like Dean myself, man! I was getting more withdrawn in myself. It wasn't that I was moody; I'd behave properly and answer when I was spoken to. But I wasn't as talkative as I was when I was a child. I used to see or hear something and instead of inquiring about it, I'd sit in my room or in a field puzzling it all out for myself. The world seemed complex to me then, but I was confident that I could sort it all out eventually.

I was continually thinking, appearing to walk about in a dream. This must have given me an air of mystery or something, because I found that it only intrigued people. At school, and I was now fifteen, it was considered an honour for me to speak to anyone, so reserved was I normally. The girls went for me in a big way but frankly I just didn't want to know about them. They were much too pointless for me; there was something else, somewhere ... I took to writing poems—kind of "Blues" songs about the things around me.

All this tightening and wondering inside me erupted towards the end of 1956. That's when a film called "Rock Around the Clock" hit Hopwich. My Mum read the papers to Dad and myself about all the rioting that was going on wherever the film was shown. This was also the Teddy Boy era and so, to Mum and Dad, it seemed a pretty dangerous proposition for me to go and see the film, but they didn't say so outright. Dad might have been happier actually if I had shown some spark of rebellion. My Mum probably worried about my long lapses into silence, but I was a hard worker and in our village that was the main thing.

So I saw this film. I didn't go on Saturday night with crowds from school, but instead slipped in on Monday evening. I sat in the circle instead of the stalls as I wanted to watch every second. I stayed for two showings, coming out after the first one to pay to see it a second time. It was a knockout. Although I wasn't too keen on the blatant exhibitionism of the dancers and what even to my unmusical ear seemed to be sheer exploitation of this new sound. I was fascinated by the individuality of the noise. And this was the time of Elvis Presley's *Heartbreak Hotel,* on the radio as well. The combined influence of the two was enough to show me exactly where my next move lay. I needed a guitar.

All the next year, I worked every hour that I could on the farm, including the long summer holiday. Mum, who banked my money because she ran the post office side of the store, used to pull my leg. But I didn't tell her what I was saving for. Both my parents were very proud of me. They watched my muscles grow and sensed the ambition burning in me as I sat in the parlour with them, maybe listening to the radio, or glancing at the *Farmers' Weekly,* or just dreaming.

I would get some fantasy in my mind, about what Bill Haley might do if he came to Thickley, for instance, and dwell on it for days. I used to dream of buying the guitar and practising it until I was perfect. Then I wanted to ask everyone to a big concert in the village hall where I would just sit on stage and let my guitar talk, thrilling the audience with my music.

But as my savings mounted, I began to feel frightened. Could I really do what I had set out to do? It's easy to dream when things aren't likely to come true. I had set myself a task and I didn't want to risk letting myself down.

In the end, the brooding erupted and I told my parents of my plans. Their reaction was immediate. They made me draw out my savings, take Saturday off from the farm, and go to Chester and buy my guitar.

CHAPTER 3

Chester is a town I have always liked, with its quaint balconies overlooking the main street. I walked along the streets for hours during the morning. Being Saturday the streets were fairly busy. In one of the big stores there I saw a fabulous pair of brown suede chukka-boots—something I had never seen before. I decided that if I had six guineas left after getting the guitar, I'd buy myself those.

The guitar was easy to find but I didn't rush in and buy it straight away. I walked up and down outside the shop, kind of torturing myself. In a few minutes I could walk into the shop and buy something which was going to change my whole life. But I wanted to delay it; I wanted to enjoy that masochistic thrill of forcing myself to wait. Probably I'm over-dramatizing things—and I was just plain scared to go in the shop; but looking back and knowing about kinks now (to a certain extent!) I guess I was naturally odd.

Anyway I bought the guitar when I'd practically wetted my pants with bolted-in excitement. It was an acoustic model, with a black plastic case, which I slung happily from my back. I went back and bought the chukka-boots which I wore. I made for the bus station. There was a bus at three which links up with the Hopwich bus to home. I couldn't wait to get back and start practising. In the shop I had casually strummed the strings, not really knowing what sounds I was making. When the fellow asked me if I wanted a plectrum I didn't know what he meant.

"Hey, how'd you like to come to a party," a voice challenged me suddenly.

I was startled. Turning, I saw a boy not much taller than me. He was wearing tight American style jeans ("Levis" he proudly told me later, "Got them from the States when I was in the Merchant") and a jean-style jacket. He had a hard face with a very thin mouth and pale blue eyes. I was nervous, not sure what he was after; maybe he had mistaken me for someone else.

If it came to a fight, I could look after myself all right—I may not have looked much then but hard work and exercise had given me all the muscles I needed. *Christ! I can't help it if I look so baby-faced and sweet!* Perhaps if I had got into a good fight then, someone would have slashed my face and I'd have a decent scar to rough me up a bit.

"It's on a boat tonight," the fellow said. "Play your guitar and no one will mind you coming along."

I smiled ruefully. "I've only just bought it; I can't play a note yet."

"Then I'll give you a few tips; I can't play well, but I know a few chords."

If there had been a hundred pounds waiting for me on the seat of my bus, I don't think I would have gone then. Here I was with a brand new guitar I had no more idea of how to play than I had of riding a motorbike, and here was someone offering to teach me. But what was stopping me? After the first few seconds, nothing. It was in those first few seconds that I was weighing up the situation.

Although I was fifteen I was still a very reserved boy and still at school. I just hadn't had any experience with strangers. And this was one who'd stopped me in the street and whose face I wasn't sure that I could trust. That was the last time I ever felt those first few moments of indecision whenever I met anyone new. From then on I became insatiable for strangers who said they'd be able to help me, *or buy me a drink!*

I looked up at Randy, as he later said he was called. "Okay then," I said, "let's go."

He was twenty, and used to be a steward in the Merchant Navy. That's where he learnt to play the guitar. He was working on the buildings, he told me, but he went round with all sorts of people. This party he had mentioned was being given by some society type girl he knew who had hired a barge to take everyone up the River Dee for the night. There'd be lots of booze and it should be a good time, if I wanted to go.

We came to Randy's house. It was by the canal, the "cut" as he called it. It was a tiny cottage sandwiched between others as equally dilapidated. To reach it we had to scramble down a mud-bank at the side of a small bridge and on to the tow-path. The front door was about five feet away from the water's edge. Randy joked about the number of times he and his mates had fallen in. Every night when he came home pissed he fell in, even after living there for a year. It was one way of sobering him up, though, before he had to face his wife.

As he pushed open his front door, I saw her. She was sitting on a settee in front of a basket of dirty nappies. A kid about two was scrambling round the floor, while she was changing the nappy of a tiny baby on her lap. The room itself was very small, with a steep staircase leading out of it to whatever chaos there was upstairs. A torn plastic curtain screened off the kitchen area. The room smelled of the damp which glistened on the walls. Randy was proud of his home, which he had bought for a hundred pounds to live in for a couple of years until it was demolished. His wife, a charming unaffected girl, obviously well used to Randy's chatter, greeted me casually and went on changing the baby.

Randy sat down on the table and examined my guitar. He was impressed. And then, in those bizarre surroundings, with the kid tugging my trousers and wanting me to play with him, I had my first ever guitar lesson. It was six cups of tea, some bread and jam, and five hours later that we finished. Randy had shown me all he knew, including the words of a dozen or so American folk songs. I just wouldn't let him stop once he'd started turning that guitar into a living instrument.

Fortunately, Randy himself was so starved of an audience and someone he could obviously impress that he didn't mind a bit. Mind you, I didn't learn half of what he told me. I was so excited—in a calm, calculating way—that I just couldn't take it all in. But I did pick up chord changes, and learnt how to manipulate my fingers. And, most important of all to me, Randy professed to be knocked out by my playing, he reckoned I was a natural.

It was his wife who pointed out the time. She wanted to

put the television on, and would we kindly move, or preferably belt up. I hadn't seen television very often, and would have liked to watch it. Then I realized that I was stranded in Chester for the night! I didn't know what to do. My parents would be pretty worried.

"We may as well go to the party, then," said Randy.

We went first to a pub in one of the balconies overlooking the street. It was full of types of people I'd never met before—kind of bohemian young conservatives. They were dressed in hacking jackets and cavalry twill trousers and spoke loudly and arrogantly like intellectual teddy boys. I didn't like them. Instead Randy took me to another pub, which had a juke box and a more genuine collection of customers—most of them wore the draped jackets and drainpipe trousers associated with hooligans. We finished up at a pub on the riverside. All this time we were drinking, although Randy had to order because I was under age, and looked it, too. I was drinking halves of bitter, like him.

At the riverside pub, there were crowds of posh people trying to get with it. I couldn't stand them and, said Randy, neither could he. He just mixed with them because it helped him, he said.

"How?" I asked him, very puzzled.

"Because I'm a builder's labourer without any talent for anything except I look good," he said. "These people like me because I'm from a different world to them; they cultivate me, buy me drinks, and in return I entertain them with my chat. They may even put work my way, like a decorating job. And I get their girls as well, though they don't know about that. And I hear the gossip—I find out where I can make a few quid quickly.

"Take my advice—if you want to get on at anything, you've got to move out of your own background. You've got to do things and mix with people you don't even like; you've got to be disciplined, one step ahead of the next man; you even have to be phoney, have sex with people you can't stand, yeah even men—but you'll get there in the end. The big time."

Suddenly everyone started moving. A girl grabbed my hand and pulled me along with her. I was bundled, far too abandoned to protest, into the barge and onto another girl's lap. She put her arms round me, cradling me like a doll. I know I was small, but this was ridiculous.

One of the intellectuals came over and rescued me with a bottle of beer. I didn't think I could take any more beer, but it was an excuse to get off the girl's lap. I went over to the side and sat down by myself as the barge pulled away from the shore. I had no idea where we were going, I wasn't even sure who I was at that particular moment.

As we pulled away from the lights of the shore, it got very dark on board. There was shouting and screaming and laughing and, as someone had brought a radio, it wasn't long before the boat was swaying with people jiving. I took a long swig of beer to help me cope and promptly became more confused. Someone—it must have been Randy—asked if I was all right.

I was contemplating a very ornate ceiling. It was white I distinctly remember, with bunches of plaster grapes standing out in relief. There was a red glow from a lamp somewhere over to the right, on the floor probably. I groaned, and from somewhere by my navel, a woman's voice spoke, her hot breath tingling my naked stomach.

I sat up abruptly. There was a girl with her head—a mass of beautiful blonde ringlets—in my lap. She raised her head slowly, looking at me with bleary eyes. We were lying on a settee in a fantastic room. I had never seen furniture so expensive or exquisite. But I was in too much of a panic to think of that.

I saw I'd still got most of my clothes on. My new chukka boots and jacket were on the floor, and my shirt had been pulled open. The girl who was with me looked around twenty-three (in actual fact, as I discovered four years later, she was sixteen). She gave me a silly smile, and tried to kiss my nose. I turned away puzzled. She kissed my chest then buried her head in my lap again.

"Where's Randy?" I asked, groping for the slender lifeline

my consciousness provided. My head was aching terribly. I regretted ever having had a drink.

"He's upstairs, of course," said the girl.

I eased myself away from her and got up off the settee. There was a massive oak chest against one wall, with several bottles on it, I fancied something long and cool –anything to get rid of the muzziness in my head. There was no beer, only spirits and French stuff.

I chose a thick green bottle of what I thought was cordial. It was a yellowish liquid and smelt of peppermint. I half filled my glass with it and then went in search of some water. There was a jug on a table by the settee. I poured the water in and the yellowish liquid turned to green. At first I thought it was me. I drank the stuff straight down without noticing the taste. It seemed refreshing, so I went back for another slug. It was called Pernod.

The next time I woke up I was on a different settee. The ceiling above my eyes, which seemed to be stuck on long girders at the foot of a quarry which had just been blasted, was flaking. There were damp patches of brown on the wallpaper. I wasn't alone. Randy, completely naked, lay beside me. My trousers and my Y-fronts were around my knees.

I jumped off the settee quickly. A mallet slammed down on my head, cracking me back. I tried more slowly. This time it was just a continual swish and slap of a cow's tail when she gets niggly during milking. I stood up blindly, trying to make out if all my limbs were there. As I opened my eyes again, to accustom them to the morning which was shrieking in through the window, I caught sight of my beloved guitar. I immediately felt a bit better, although deeply ashamed at the things I could only dimly recall having done. I pulled up my trousers, zipped the guitar into its case, slung it over my shoulder, and fled.

The next day I went back to school, spending the evenings practising instead of on the farm. A few weeks later, I left school and started work.

♦ ♦ ♦ ♦ ♦

There was another boy in the village who was keen on rock and skiffle; the two popular forms of music then. We soon found a boy at the youth club who wanted to be a drummer, and together decided to form the Thickley Skiffle Group. We met every possible night in the old barn down Thickley Lane, when it wasn't too dark or cold.

Sometimes the vicar let us use Thickley Hall, although he didn't really approve of our style of music, saying it was for hooligans. He did recognize, though, the important fact that we were doing something creative ourselves and in that respect should be encouraged. This two-faced attitude to music was something I couldn't understand but was to come up against in various forms throughout my time in show-business—particularly with cinema managers who really hated my guts but liked the money I brought in.

I taught Geoff and Tom, the other two members of the skiffle group, the songs I had learnt from Randy. They were really Negro (blues) songs, and I liked the feel of them. That's how I became the singer of the group. Without anyone to actually teach us, we were very imitative of anything we heard on radio concentrating on the rhythm and blues and country and western items, buying only records with the sound I liked. I wasn't dead keen on rock, preferring music which echoed what I thought to be a genuine feeling of people rather than stereotyped pop music.

I get my worst nightmares in bed here with a pop rock background—that terrible and uninspired beat typical of the state of pop music from the time people like Presley dropped off and I came on the scene. Those dreadful dirges drove pop into the doldrums then: it's a wonder teenagers didn't swing right back to Johnny Ray and Malcolm Vaughan.

Now I know that if I had been born in Russia I would have been the perfect young Russian, such was my dedication to that guitar and my ideology. Of course, the music I wanted to play wasn't really Russian, but I'm sure that if I had lived in Russia and shown the flair I obviously had, I would have been slapped into a school to devote my life to music. And I'd have liked that. Not that it was any strain playing the guitar in the evenings and working on the farm by day. It was only later that this interest grew into an obsession which conflicted with my work.

The boys and I worked out an act which we used to feature at clubs and dances surrounding our village. We sung our own compositions whenever we could, but had to concentrate a lot on the current hits. Through us, the local kids came a step nearer to the big time idols, although we were just like them ourselves really. The parents who frowned on our activities overlooked one important fact: we were having a ball in the good old fashioned way—making our own entertainment. We were also getting fans. Jill was one of them.

Jill was, and still is, the only girl I have ever really loved. Since her I have slept with dozens of girls and I'd be a very strange teenage idol if I hadn't. But no one has taken the place of Jill—mainly because I've forgotten the power to love.

Poking different women all the time, just obliging that little urge of lust inside one, soon takes the essential mystery out of love. I guess that's why I don't still love Jill, but can dimly remember having loved her. There was the usual attraction, of course, but there was also something stronger, and innocent.

She came from a different social background. Her father was a Liverpool businessman, and drove one of the Jaguars which snorted through Thickley every morning and evening. I watched her at dances several times, wondering if I'd ever pluck up courage to talk to her. I did eventually, of course, and asked her if she'd care to walk out with me the following Sunday afternoon. She accepted!

No one took us seriously because we both looked like children. Jill was weak through illness and didn't seem to be gaining strength. The village which had watched me grow from a tousled-haired angelic kid, to a lanky-haired pleasant-looking teenager, didn't see much maturity about me. But Jill and I treated our affair with all the fervour of teenage passion.

My sixteenth birthday heralded an idyllic year. I had my job on the farm that I enjoyed and I was earning good money; I had a girl friend who loved me; and I had a hobby which made me and others happy. My own love for Jill was growing stronger and it seemed inevitable that we should marry, although neither of us mentioned that.

I woke up crying this morning as I remembered her kisses: pure beautiful kisses, unlike the monster caresses of sexual embrace.

As time wore on, I got to thinking in my own limited way just what I wanted out of life. In spite of Jill, the guitar was becoming an obsession with me. I had been working on the farm for nearly two years, by then and playing for longer than that. What had I got to show for it? Why! I hadn't even seen much more than a ten mile radius of Thickley. Although the locals liked me, I didn't even know if I was any good as a guitarist or if my songs were worth much.

I knew from the discovery of such people as Tommy Steele, that it was possible for an ordinary boy, yes, just like me, to succeed in show business if he wanted to. Not that I wanted to, but I was beginning to feel slightly hemmed in by all that was happening in Thickley. I still wanted to play the guitar, but I wanted to improve. My dedication was such that I knew I needed more practical knowledge instead of listening to records all the time. I remembered what Randy had told me, to escape from my background.

I didn't mention any of this to Jill, of course, but kept it bottled up inside me. Maybe this is what made our caresses more violent, more demanding. We were both well aware of our feelings when we were together and our difficulty in controlling them.

It was the end of the harvest season when it happened. I had been working hard for weeks and had rarely seen Jill at all, except if she came down in the evenings to bring me a snack. On the last night there was to be a small celebration at the farm house. I didn't fancy it myself. Since Chester, I had rarely touched much drink, apart from the occasional beer to refresh myself in the fields during the day. I didn't see the point in drinking when Jill was waiting for me.

We walked slowly down Thickley Lane. My sun-tanned body was glistening where the sweat still hadn't dried on my skin. My jeans and shirt stuck comfortably to me. Jill, her face blissful and content as we walked along arm in arm, had never looked more desirable to me than then. I was tired after the long day, but in the dusk with her, a new vitality swept through me. There was a strange surging in my thighs, which I couldn't explain.

We turned off the lane without saying a word. I led her, my muscled arm gently around her shoulder, to the old barn. A rat scurried in front of us; Jill, bless her, didn't notice but kept her huge eyes fixed adoringly on me. We were both living a dream. Her delicate arm wound round my body, under my shirt as I pulled her closer to me. That kiss had a sweetness I had never tasted before. It went on forever.

Slowly we sunk to the ground, my arm acting as a pillow for her head as we devoured each other. My strong hands were playing her body in a way I never meant to; I could feel her fluttering response as she pressed herself closer, even closer, to me. We were locked in each other's arms, naked, blissfully marvelling at the strength and demands of our bodies. Slowly I made love to her. We were both virgins, both inexperienced, but nothing could have bettered the perfection of that evening.

The next day my penis throbbed and ached as though on fire, my balls had a lead weight attached to them, and my mind kept on re-enacting every thrust. I didn't go to Church.

CHAPTER 4

The Jaguar sped along the A41 to Liverpool. Outside it was wintry, the trees were leafless now, and a pall of crisp frost covered the earth. Cattle had been bedded in the barns for the winter, and the countryside was hibernating. In the car it was warm and comfortable with an intimate peace enveloping Jill and myself. I held her hand underneath the tartan travelling rug wrapped round our legs. Her head was lolling towards my shoulder; soon she would be snuggling up to me. I stared ahead, not taking much notice of the thin red neck of her father as he steered the car. I was lost in one of my dreams again. Jill's mother, looking ridiculous to me in her blue hat shaped like an upturned bucket, turned and smiled at us.

We were going to Liverpool so that Jill could visit her aunt there for the weekend. It had taken quite a lot to persuade me to go along with her, as I was still very doubtful about mixing with adult society, especially anyone so formidable as Jill's parents. But Jill was insistent. She said it would give us all an opportunity to get to know each other. We would stay at her aunt's that night and return the next day so I wouldn't miss much on the farm. I insisted on taking the guitar. Jill just laughed, said there wouldn't be any chance for me to play it—her aunt only liked classical music.

Actually, our real reason for going to Liverpool was so that we could sleep together. Since that evening in September, we had not had much chance for making love. The colder evenings meant we couldn't hang around in the open for long, and the close intimacy of life in our own homes, with parents forever in the way, restricted anything but the mildest love-play. There were two occasions however, when both Jill's parents were away from home at the same time. It was a simple matter to get the housekeeper out to the pub. Then, timing it so we wouldn't be interrupted, we quickly made love, usually on the floor in front of Jill's settee with the television blazing away, me keeping an ear open for guitarists.

That was an unhappy state of affairs but Jill herself looked much better, she suddenly began to fill out and looked radiant. Her parents were convinced that the country air was doing the trick. They certainly didn't have an inkling of our real relationship. My parents, on the other hand, were shrewder. They noticed the change in me, the effect Jill was having. It was Dad who gave me a diplomatic warning about not trying to rush things, and to remember that we were all in God's hands, and why didn't I go to church anymore.

But what made me unhappy about Jill and myself was this clandestine bit. It even seemed to put a slur on our friendship when we had to calculate and plot for when we could make love.

This was the latest of Jill's plans and, frankly, I was getting disgusted with it. I didn't want sex to rule my life. (*Then!*) I had my job and my guitar, Jill had nothing. Although we probably had sex only three or four times before this Liverpool trip, it sickened me so much (although at the time I enjoyed it, of course) that I was even more nervous with Jill's parents than I should have been.

Another outcome of that evening behind the old barn had been quite unforeseen. For some time there had been this tension in me as I contemplated my own future and obligations on the farm. Jill had provided a release. I suppose what had really happened is that I was on the way to becoming a man both physically and mentally now that I had lost my virginity.

It's a subject which isn't often referred to, but I'm sure the loss of a man's virginity is just as important to him as the loss of a girl's is to her. Yet it shouldn't be mentioned as though "losing" virginity is a crime—it's the most beautiful act I know. It's a kind of gaining a new dimension. It seems to me to be a cockeyed moral system of ours when boys are always boasting of having had sex, when they probably haven't, and girls are always saying they haven't had it when they probably have. I must ask my nurse what she thinks.

In those days, thoughts like that hadn't reached my innocent, narrow, little mind. All I knew then was that the girl who was squeezing my hand affectionately, yes, the girl I loved was about to involve me in a plot which my mind said was wrong but which my body wasn't strong enough to resist. Her calculating ways were sabotaging our relationship.

Yeah? And what about me? If I had been going to marry her I should have proposed long before that, and taken the upper hand in our relationship, making her do things my way. Instead, I was so weak I just let myself be led along. She's probably married to a prosperous tycoon now, the darling of Merseyside Society.

At Jill's aunts, after all the introductions and chat, I did a curious thing. Suddenly, I just had to get away. I excused myself and went out into the street. Luckily my guitar was still in the boot of the Jag. I had a feeling I needed it with me, more as a friend than for any practical reason. I was now alone in a city I had only visited as a kid a couple of times.

I found my way to the centre of town. It was only then that it occurred to me that I was rather an obvious figure in my best, in fact only, suit with a guitar slung over my back. But they must have been used to that sort of thing in Liverpool, for no one made any comments. I looked around for a cafe wanting to find friends, to express myself.

Down Tater Street, not far from the Empire, I saw a place called the Panda. It wasn't one of these pseudo-smart Italianised coffee bars, notable only for the high prices, poor food and complete lack of atmosphere. This looked different. I went in, and another piece of the jig-saw fitted into place.

Inside it was a bit like a workmen's cafe; distempered walls and ceiling with pew-like benches round the chipped Formica-topped tables. A juke box was belting out the latest pop tunes, and the whole place was steaming with teenagers. The atmosphere in the place was electrifying. With all those people I wasn't quite sure what to do. Like a moth, I made straight for the bright lights of the juke box, planning to survey the room from there.

The kids in the corner looked very friendly, many of them nodded to me as though they'd seen me before. It must have been the guitar. Heading for the juke box, I realized where the counter was, and pushed myself through the crowd to get a coke. The girl behind the counter looked at my guitar and smiled.

"You're a bit early," she said.

Mystified, I walked away. The record being played wasn't one of the latest hits after all, but
an early rhythm-and-blues disc from America. I was fascinated. It was almost as though I'd come home. Then it struck me that all city cafés may have been like that, since I'd not been around very much, and never to Liverpool.

Someone was talking to me out of the mass of faces. This face, a boy's, was crowned with a shock of unruly fair hair. Maybe it was the atmosphere of the place which had set my mind flashing back, but to me this kid looked just like James Dean.

"Hi, whack," he was saying in a thicker accent than mine. Haven't seen you around here before."

We couldn't talk very much in that crowd, so he led me through a pass door into a tiny office beyond. He introduced himself as Vincent and said he was a drummer.

"We play here every night," he said. "Downstairs. What about you?"

He was an easy person to speak to. He was a lot more intelligent than I was, at least better educated. He said he was at the Art College, but had just joined up with a group to play in the evenings. I found myself pouring my heart out to him about my beloved guitar and the sort of music I liked to play, how I wrote my own songs, and yet how I was frightened because I had no yardstick to judge my efforts by.

Vincent could hardly contain himself. He was leaping up and down off the desk back to the floor then pacing backwards and forwards as I talked. His excitement was infectious. I was flushed when I'd finished speaking. I had talked myself into tackling the world.

"Come on," said Vincent, tugging at my arm when I'd finished. "I'm going to show you a few things."

He hustled me out of the café with him. We were almost

running as we went up Tater Street away from the main road. We crossed over a few back streets and then we were there—in front of a huge luxurious block of flats.

"This is where I live," said Vincent. He must have seen the gasp of astonishment on my face, for he was a scruffy looking kid with paint stained jeans and black leather jacket. I felt a bit annoyed—I didn't know he was rich, just thought he was a normal fellow like myself. I certainly wouldn't have confided in him if I'd known. Vincent just laughed, and led me through the posh entrance and up the deep-pile carpeted stairs. I had that feeling of being exhibited as some sort of freak all over again, just as happened in Chester.

He gave four sharp rings on the door to his flat. I wanted to go, find my way back to Jill, dear Jill. She must have been frantic then wondering where I'd gone. I hadn't intended to be out this long. I'd just say that I couldn't stop and then go. Vincent had caught hold of my arm again, ready to steer me in.

I was ready for the worst when the door opened but not for this. Before us stood a girl in bra and panties, nothing else. She had Brigitte Bardot lips, maybe that's what gave her the right to walk about like that. She pulled me in, then we had to wait for the door to be closed before we could walk any further.

The hallway was stacked on both sides with canvasses, easels, lumps of rock and clay chipped into weird shapes. The wallpaper was splattered with splodges of oil paint. Thanks to the destructive enthusiasm of a wild group of beatniks who evidently lived there, the luxury of this particular flat was a myth.

Vincent chuckled, leading me into the front room. The girl disappeared somewhere else. I was amazed. There were three mattresses strewn about the bare boards of the floor. Each had an assortment of tattered bedclothes on them and a boy, similarly dressed to Vincent. He kind of merged into the room, being difficult to distinguish from the filth and chaos. The only light came from a red bulb stuck high up in the ceiling. As though to make the ceiling lower, someone had draped gauze from wall to wall, and this filtered the light to almost total darkness. Piles of books and paintings were everywhere.

In the far corner, running alongside one wall was a cup-board-like piece of furniture which turned out to be two home-made bunks. A clothes line tacked along the other wall supported various hangers with the limited, but entire wardrobe of the four inhabitants of this room. They were in-troduced by Vincent as being the rest of the Rhythmettes, as they called themselves—Brian, Po, and Husk, all guitarists by night and art students by day—if ever they managed to get up from the pile of rags they were pleased to call their beds.

In an atmosphere like that, of sheer squalor but splen-did easy-going happiness, I was surprised to feel quite at home. The boys said they lived in the flat which they'd taken unfurnished, because it was cheaper than anywhere else. Most nights there were about ten of them sleeping in the three bedrooms, kitchen and bathroom and sharing the rent of ten guineas a week. There were always other bums who just dropped in and sometimes contributed something. It was a glorious communal atmosphere, and I fell for the set-up straight away, although my instincts wrinkled a bit at the dirt and foulness of the air.

There was a glow in the room from the record player which throbbed with a Negro blues shouter whilst Vincent told the rest of the Rhythmettes how he'd found me in the Panda. I could see what was coming. If I felt nervous at all, the boys helped me forget it. They were even more keen on playing than I was. It didn't take long for me to strum the guitar and an impromptu session started up.

We were really swinging and for the first time in my life I felt I could actually communicate with other people. My guitar was talking for me, and theirs were answering back. It was Po who suggested I join them at the Panda that evening. All thoughts of Jill had left me now.

The Panda then was about the only coffee bar of its kind in Liverpool bringing live beat to its patrons. Now, with Merseyside Beat an established sound in England's record business, there are at least a dozen clubs offering their home grown music. And there are about three hundred groups around there now, although maybe only 150 actually working. In *Disc* at the beginning of 1963, three years after the sound really began, a writer referred to the Liverpool beat scene as a "scene packed with rhythm and blues of a special original kind". Well, I'm proud to say that I was in there at the beginning. Even though it was just coincidence.

The Rhythmettes now are one of the top groups in the business. I made it sooner than they did, I know, but I reckon they'll last longer than I did. They should certainly be more used to the carve-ups and dangers of the beat game than I was, for they've been around. If they can get away with playing in strip clubs, gambling joints and those wild German beer haunts they've been in without being too affected, they'll last anything. It took them three years to reach the top which must have helped keep them level headed, and they had each other to deflate them, or cheer them up if things got too tough. I'm not looking for excuses, now, but I had none of those advantages.

The Rhythmettes played in the cellar under the Panda. It was a well-equipped gaff with a microphone and a small dais for the group. The unplastered bricks had been whitewashed and, when it was empty, the place had a stark air about it in spite of the green and red lights. The boys, although they had only been playing for a few months, already had a hard core of fans. It was these and their friends who jammed that cellar to capacity. Occasionally someone tried to dance but it was practically impossible. After the first half hour, Brian announced me over the microphone. The change in singing style was slow to register but gradually the fact that there was a newcomer on stage seeped through to the kids.

I was both nervous and excited at having this chance to perform before a new audience as I started my first number. I did a straight rhythm and blues piece, styled almost word for word on the American version I had heard on record.

Then I tried some of my own numbers with the boys doing spontaneous harmonizing. It was as if I could do nothing wrong that evening. The kids in the cellar caught the feeling we were putting into those numbers. They didn't try to dance, they hardly talked, they just listened to me, a young lad like themselves, singing his heart out with words they understood. I was mobbed; it was a fantastic success.

As I came off the dais, leaving the Rhythmettes to wind up the evening, my mind was in a complete whirl. Hands reached for me from all parts of the cellar, voices babbled in my ear. "That was gear . . . hey, what's your name? . . . fabulous! . . . are you coming tomorrow?"

I made for the stairs, confused and happy. There was a huge man there with a great black beard. He leaned out over the heads of the girls milling around me, and grabbed me roughly by the shoulder. He pulled me towards the stairs, out of their reach. It turned out that he was the owner of the Panda, liked my singing and wanted me to come again with the Rhythmettes some evenings.

The Rhythmettes took me back to their flat that night. Well, not straight away. We went onto a party first. I had been warned by my first escapade about what happens at parties. I drank sparingly and most of the time kept in conversation with Husk. He was a quiet boy like myself. When Vincent said he could fix me up with a girl for the night if I wanted one, Husk seemed to understand my refusal without me having to explain. Even if I hadn't got Jill, whom I suddenly remembered with a shudder for running out on her, I didn't want a girl for that night, nor ever again. It was just me and my guitar from now on!

In the flat, we talked about the evening. Brian absentmindedly fondling the girl lying on the mattress with him, was struggling to express himself.

"You were good, Dan; too good for us. You see, you're a striking character; well, look at you. The birds were going nuts tonight. They like us, but they've never gone that mad. I reckon you're going to make it big, really big. We've had an experience tonight; almost seen a star being born. You're

34

going to make it, but you'll make it by yourself —you don't need us or anyone like us. You've got it already."

Po interrupted, drawing heavily on a cigarette. "You sound as though you're running him down, man. Brian's just jealous. He knows we can't teach you anything new."

"It amazes me that you could have done so much just stuck out in Thickley," said Vincent. "You're obviously a natural."

"He's been working along the same lines as us, that's all," said Brian again. "While we've been all fugged up with college, Dan's been out in the fields letting the fresh air blow some cool thinking in his mind. Giving him new ideas which he's mixed with what he's heard on disc. Isn't that right, kid?"

I didn't know what to say. I just listened to them, strumming my guitar softly in the background, hoping they'd keep on talking. I'd never heard anyone discuss music—especially my music—before.

"He's still a natural, though, I reckon," defended Vincent. "He's got to work out just where he's going. I mean do you want to make the big time or not?"

I shrugged. They obviously expected an answer. I felt a new kind of intoxication: it elated me. "Big time? I don't know, I just don't know," I muttered. "It's just that I'm eaten up by this desire to play."

"That's fine," said Husk, swigging quietly at a bottle of beer. "If you ever start playing for money, I reckon you've had it. Just play because you enjoy it, and you'll be all right. It won't matter if you don't make the big time."

"But it helps," broke in Brian. "It's no good playing all your life and no one digging you. And the more people who dig you, the better. That's why presentation is so important. It's no good just the music being good, you've got to look good, act good, as well. That's what I meant before—this kid's got all that. Mind you, he needs to learn a lot in other directions." He winked at Vincent, who, like Brian and Po, had also got girls with them.

So the discussion continued for a while, on musical

themes, on ambitions, on instruments, on records. Then the words got less and the remarks more pointed towards sleep. Husk got up from his lonely corner where he had been squatting on an old beer crate, and made for the bunks. "You take the top one, kid," he told me quickly stripping down to his pants and climbing in the bottom bunk. I followed suit, nearly pulling the whole contraption over as I clambered on top. The other three boys were already engrossed in their birds.

It took me ages to get to sleep that night. My brain was racing jerkily along two tracks: Jill and music. I pictured Jill in bed at her aunt's, heartbroken by my disappearance. I didn't feel too good about it either, but I had a decision now—my music was going to come first. Jill, love, sex, weren't important. I had learned a lot by this evening with the Rhythmettes. The main question was what was I going to do next? The big time? It was a big world but these boys at least thought I had the talent.

Sleep came to me in time to save me the embarrassment of hearing the sighs and wheezing body-music of three teenage Rhythmettes copulating on the floor.

CHAPTER 5

The next weeks were tiresome ones. I was waiting for my eighteenth birthday—just three years ago - when it was agreed I could leave Thickley for London, in search of the big time. Dad wanted me to wait a bit in case I changed my mind. Also, to please my parents, I said I would come back in three months if I didn't get anywhere.

The weeks were spent arranging for me to stay with an aunt in Hertfordshire, and in me being given all sorts of advice on looking after myself. I also had to point out to Jill that I still loved her but had to go because of what was going through my mind. She couldn't understand how a guitar could be a substitute for her.

If I'd known better perhaps I would have told her that the guitar wasn't a substitute at all. It was a job, a career which I wanted to follow and it was just that it required so much concentration that she would have to be excluded from my life for the time being.

Thinking of what eventually happened, I get stricken with remorse at the glib way I threw Jill over, only to forget my dedication and replace her with dozens of others. I don't know where she is now, but if she ever reads this book, I hope she'll forgive me.

If my parents and Jill couldn't quite understand why I wanted to go to London, I'm not certain that I did. To me, London was paved with gold, heaven-on-earth. I felt sure that it would be in London that I'd find the reason for going there. I wasn't after fame or fortune—just seeking a chance to change my life, to sing and play and to learn more.

I wasn't really thinking of "the big time." I reckoned that I would get a job as a guitarist eventually if I was as good as people said. I wanted to seek out the top names, rub shoulders with them, and see how they did it. I suppose I could have gone to Liverpool instead but that wasn't London. How many times, I wonder, has the traditional magic of London proved traumatically tragic as it lured provincial youngsters like myself to their doom?

My birthday was on a Saturday. There was no celebration. That night, I took Jill for a last walk. We talked most of the time about what it would be like in London, about all the girls I'd meet up there, and how, said Jill, I'd soon forget her. She said she'd wait and still be there in three months if I returned.

I promised to write but even then I suppose she knew I wouldn't. She told me to be careful, and was almost in tears at the thought of me, her sweet lovable Dan with his long blond hair and innocent grin, struggling to survive in ruthless London.

She kept on throwing her arms round me and moaning, saying how she wanted to cuddle me for always and always and not to go, please don't go. Her tears almost made me cry. I was glad to break away from that last kiss outside her home. I didn't want to leave her arms either, but this sort of farewell only made it worse. And I had to go.

She turned away from me and ran up the path to her front door. I could hear her sobs from where I stood in the shadow of the oak trees overhanging the lane. She opened the front door quickly and went in without looking back. That was the last time I saw her.

I went to Church with Mum and Dad on Sunday morning and enjoyed it—not that I was ever a very religious boy. It was just a tradition like Sunday lunch and Billy Cotton on the radio, which made Sunday's complete and a contrast from the rest of the week. My parents felt that as long as I went to church, I would remain as good, kind and gentle as I looked. It seems a pity that the time I wasted singing hymns and making obeisance to a kinky old vicar wasn't spent preparing myself for the buffeting I was going to receive in later years.

My aunt lived in a council house at the far end of Todworth, near Watford. She had been evacuated with her husband and family during the war. Although they wanted to, they had never had the chance to get back to West Ham.

The first thing about my new home I noticed was the toilet. At least I wouldn't have to walk down the garden like at home. And it was a flush one, too.

My aunt was taller than my mother, and had much more of a brash attitude about her. She positively towered above me, although she did seem to get shorter as I got to know her. My uncle was a stocky man with a ginger moustache. He was a fitter with a local firm. They had two children, a son who was in the army and daughter still at school. It was arranged that I should sleep in the bedroom of my cousin, the soldier.

It took me a few days to settle in with this new way of life. I was used to going to bed early and getting up early; to being alone with myself and not having to talk. I must have been a strange contrast to my cousin who was a typical suburban boy, all chat and fancy clothes.

On Saturdays, Todworth exploded with a jazz club. Although I didn't dig jazz at all I went along just to see what the local teenagers were like. I missed having someone to talk to the way I used to talk to Jill. In fact, I was beginning to wonder if I'd done the right thing in coming to London. My reaction hadn't been so immediate as had my mother's when she first arrived in Thickley. This was the same process in reverse about twenty years later, and it wasn't working so well at all.

At the jazz club, as fate seemed to have planned, I met John. John figures constantly in my life from now on, so it's as well to get a proper picture of him. At the time I had no idea what his feelings were for me—it's only now that I can guess his motives in chatting to me that night.

But if a fellow has a friend who does for him half as much as John has done for me then he's got a real mate. If John could have known the sacrifices he was going to make for me, I wonder if he would have come up and chatted to me that evening after all. (He's just nodded "yes", because he's sitting on the bed beside me with the tape recorder.)

The steady thump of the trad-band and the heaving mass of skipping jivers, arms flaying out in all directions, in their weird beatnik clothes, were all fascinating. I felt sorry for those kids in a way, public school exhibitionists with Daddy's car outside. But as I got to know the jazz club crowd more during the next few weeks, I discovered that they were a fairly mixed bunch. Only a few of them had the affectations which make some young people with their puffed-up opinions of themselves, unbearable.

Pushing through the melee of jivers in front of me, was a boy about my age. He had dark crinkly hair cut very short and was neatly dressed with a white shirt, red tie and dark jacket. I noticed this idly, merely because he was coming in my direction. He had a goatee-type beard sprouting on his chin and, apart from that, seemed the sort of boy who wouldn't look out of place at our club in Thickley.

He looked a bit peaky of course, being a town lad. He must have caught my quick glance at him, for he smiled back at me saying something which I couldn't hear above the raucous pounding of the Saturday night trad men. I just shrugged, as though I had heard. That wasn't enough for him. He leant down to my ear and muttered some pleasantry about not having seen me there before.

Maybe I was a bit homesick and lonely, for I soon found myself in the pub across the road, sitting at a corner table, answering John's questions. He was an assistant in the film library at Pinewood Studios; lived, we discovered, a few streets away from my aunt; knew my cousin, Steve, very well; drove a scooter, liked me a lot; and how about me coming down to the Swan for a drink tomorrow lunch-time?

John struck me as being a very controlled and sensible person. He was younger than me, only seventeen, but obviously knew a lot more about life; he had a certain assurance which I found both impressive and embarrassing. I didn't like letting him order the drinks all the time. I felt I ought to make the effort but when I did offer, I must have mumbled so quietly and indecisively that it riled him.

John was brisk and efficient, knew what he wanted. That impressed me and I reckoned I could learn from him. Maybe some of his confidence would brush off on me. I was flattered that someone like him should seek me out. And on top of all that he played drums!

That John was going to become a firm friend of mine seemed obvious even to me.

I got to the Swan early next morning hoping to talk to him about the two of us playing together. But I hadn't bargained for Sunday sessions at the Swan. The pub was packed with young people everywhere. John was surrounded by his friends. He introduced me briefly, someone offered me a drink and then I found that I was ignored whilst John kept on with his story about the party he had been to the night before. There was obviously going to be no chance to talk to him this time. I began to think perhaps I had made a rash judgement in thinking we could be friends.

The next evening I spent in London. I had already been in Todworth a week, and felt I should start exerting myself. Because of the reputation it has got as being the place for would-be singers to go to, I made my way to the Two I's in Old Compton Street. This is a strange coffee bar, and it seems incredible that rock and skiffle music in Britain was born there.

On the ground floor it is a bit like the sort of milk bars in Hopwich, apart from the huge juke-box in the window and the photographs of the stars who have been discovered or appeared there. In the basement, a group of three guitarists and a drummer were belting out hit-tunes of the moment. I watched, not very impressed, aware that I could do a lot better than them.

As can be imagined, London at night was something completely fascinating and alien to me. I crept about looking, I suppose, like a startled fawn caught in a herd of charging elephants. I hated it, everyone seemed to have somewhere to go, or someone with them. I dived into a pub in Dean Street for a drink. This was the first time I wanted a drink to relieve imagined pressures. That's why I remember the occasion pretty well. The pub I had chosen was just as packed as the street outside, but at least people weren't rushing everywhere.

It seemed a favourite haunt of writers with their green

shirts, maroon ties, check jackets and long hair. I learned later that it is renowned as a haunt of poets and perverts. Although a few heads watched me as I ordered, I felt a bit more at ease there. I gulped down my half-pint then left. On the way to Piccadilly Station I managed to call in at three other pubs. At the last one I had a double whisky. I arrived home that night, after a few drinks in Todworth, pissed.

Fortunately for me, just as my determination was being sabotaged by the despair of not getting anywhere, John took me under his wing. His drumming wasn't anything more than an affectation; he used to play bongo-drums at parties to amuse the girls—that sort of thing. However, having another musician of sorts with me I was beginning to feel more confident.

John came round to my aunt's a few evenings and I played my whole repertoire, which was quite big now; pops, hits, blues, rock and country and western numbers. John was excited and said he reckoned that together we could form a group to play for local dances. I was all for it. Within a few days he had found another guitarist to come in with us, a fellow called Paddy. I can't even remember his proper name. Paddy had a stylish guitar, and within a few weeks I had invested most of my savings into a better one for myself as well.

I can see now through my own methods that John was an old hand at making acquaintances; he merely adapted the technique he used on women, playing every move carefully until he had developed the relationship to its peak. Then he would withdraw and concentrate on someone else. Maybe that's what he intended doing with me once he had exhausted my possibilities as a likeable fellow whose dependence on him helped his ego. If he did, it never worked out that way, and that serves him right!

John took me round London, pointing out the sort of clubs and coffee bars he thought we could play in. One evening we were sweating in the cellar of one of those places when the owner, a balding conman type, announced that if anyone in the audience would like to have a go, they'd be welcome to come on stage and try. I was petrified as John pushed me forward. For one thing I hadn't got my guitar or had a rehearsal or anything.

"What do you think you've been doing for the last three-years, then," hissed John.

I got on the dais by instinct; I didn't know what I was doing. There were a few wolf-whistles from some of the louts in the crowd and that pulled me together. If they thought I looked queer then, right!—they were going to get something to make them sit up.

The lead guitarist of the group on stage, who wasn't very good anyway, let me borrow his guitar. John sat in on drums. We kept the bass and rhythm guitarists with us; they could pick up what we were doing as we went along. I opened with a straight pop number which, although not a knock-out, impressed the hundred or so kids squashed into that cellar. Then we gave them one of my numbers, a real blues-type raver. The kids lapped it up. They were shouting for more.

I was still smarting at the implied insults of those wolf-whistles, and it was the louts who'd whistled who wanted me to go on playing. But not me! I was hurt by their rudeness. I handed back the guitar to its owner who was watching me open mouthed, and walked off stage. John was amazed too but he abandoned the drums and followed me as I swept out of the cellar. That was my first show of temperament, and boy! did I feel great. Even the manager was begging me to go back. Out in the street John started rabbiting.

"What did you want to do that for, Dan? That was our big chance, and you mucked it up by walking out. Let's go back and at least see what the manager has to say. He's got lots of contacts. If he liked he could put you out on tour somewhere. So, you left them wanting more, you should live so long! You're not that big, I mean . . ."

"John," I said slowly, stopping dead still in the street, "I'm grateful to you for your friendship, and I hope you'll always give me that. But my music is my life, and I'm not going to be told what to do by you!"

I paused, aware that John was frowning at my outburst.

"I've figured something," I told him slowly. "I could play to those louts in coffee-cellars all night, but what's the point? You heard. They think I'm queer. I'm not. And if that coffee-bar conman is so helpful to singers, how come he hasn't got a big name on his books? He's just trading on blokes' ignorance."

"Er, excuse me," a voice broke in. "I heard you down in the cellar just now. I thought you were very good."

We turned, and that's how I met Peter Wickham-Smith. The bastard!

CHAPTER 6

I don't know. Are there any young people who go through life being completely normal and conventional, settling down with one girl, not having her away until after the wedding, being faithful, staying in steady jobs, buying houses, only drinking occasionally and, above all, being completely innocent and unaware of any vice or deviations ?

How can I possibly tell? I've not heard of them; I've certainly never met them or number them among my exclusive circle of friends. Appreciation of life—especially the distractions and delights of unconventional behaviour—is a heightened well-developed sense in my world, the world of the teenage idol. It's a mad chase from one stimulation to another. And I'm forced to surround myself with people like me, but I'm sure all young people aren't the same.

I wasn't at one time. This is just something that's happened. Yes, I was once an innocent chicken without the slightest knowledge or suspicion of the motives behind people's actions: of the desire in people not to help others, but to help themselves; of the evil which lurks in charitable deeds. I'm a victim of my own innocence, I suppose. Better equipped, I could have handled all the drink and sex I've had, including Wickham-Smith and his clique.

Peter Wickham-Smith was a softly spoken bachelor of thirty. He bought his clothes from Burtons, had a mother living in a bungalow at Shipton-under-Wychwood, Oxford, where he stayed most weekends; wore an obscure public school tie and worked in the Main-Philadelphia Bank, Berkeley Square, where he had been since leaving school. He spent his salary, as assistant to the manager, cautiously. Once a year he took a three-week holiday and, although he would have liked to be adventurous and visit Greece, perhaps, he went alternately to the Lake District or Cornwall with his widowed mother.

He had a modest flat in Earl's Court in a block of similarly modest flats. He preferred to eat out rather than do his own cooking, and he entertained rarely. His friends were colleagues from the bank or, thanks to his chance acquaintance with a chap he met at the Earls Court Radio Show a couple of years previously, show business managers, song writers, disc-jockeys and club owners.

This acquaintanceship with the chap, a young newsreader from a regional television station, had resulted in the two of them becoming intimate friends, with the newsreader using the studio couch in Peter's flat whenever he visited London. Being on television and having a penchant for that sort of thing, the newsreader knew a few people from the pop side of show business, whom he met when they visited his station for interviews.

One of them was Seymour Royce, the top pop songwriter of the century. And that is how the staid banker Peter Wickham-Smith came to be moving around in circles normally closed to such as he. If the flamboyant ostentatiousness of Royce and his show business cronies worried Wickham-Smith, he found consolation in the fact that, basically, these people were very similar to himself. When it came to sex, they all shared the same taste: pretty boys.

Under their influence, Wickham-Smith blossomed. The twelve years of frustration he had known since leaving school, still obvious in his tightly knit servile manner, transformed into extreme promiscuity. These new friends of his showed him how easy it was in London to get exactly what one wanted, either with promises or payment. For people of such influence in the pop field—didn't all young people want to be pop singers?—it was the easiest thing in the world to lure a boy to bed.

Many had been the times Wickham-Smith had benefited from this, with young lads being provided for him by Royce. Also, he had joined a few clubs. Some were slightly bawdy drinking clubs on second floors in Soho, others were discreet thick-piled basements where the most unexpected of well known people could be observed relaxing with others of their ilk. Most of these prominent people had good looking boys with them, although they were rarely the same boys each time.

In this atmosphere, Wickham-Smith was beginning to feel more sure of himself. He was aware however, of taking rather than giving. He had never actually made the approach to any young lad himself. He felt the time had come to do something about this, and try to repay Royce for the things he had shown him, and the boys he had put his way. And that's when he picked on me.

Of course, at the time, all I knew was that a soberly dressed man with a courteous manner, was complimenting me on the way I played and asking me and John if we'd care to join him for a coffee as he thought he might be able to help us.

We listened to his spiel. He mentioned his contacts in the pop world (the name Seymour Royce was enough to set me quaking—he had written songs and shows for every top star; he even made stars), and he thought they might be interested in me. The bastard didn't mention why.

Eventually it was arranged that I should come up to London the following evening and Wickham-Smith would see what he could do about introducing me to people. He thought it would be better if I came alone as it was essentially me as a singer he was interested in, and perhaps John would feel out of it. (That was a cool way of putting it, I must say.)

I was so chuffed at what the man was saying, I would have done anything. John smelt something odd about the idea.

"Surely, you'll want Seymour Royce to hear Dan," he said. "Well, can't we play somewhere for him?"

"I know just the thing," countered Wickham-Smith realizing he may have over-played his hand. "A friend of mine, he's a priest actually, runs a youth club in the East End for teenagers. It's a very good club, one of the best known round here. We often get top artists down to play. Thursday is the dance night, maybe you'd like to come along and do a few numbers then. I'll see if I can get Seymour down to hear you. If he likes you, you know, they'll be no looking back."

Thursday came, Seymour Royce was there, we played and

I was an instant hit.

After we came off stage, the kids still shouting for more, Peter Wickham-Smith brought Royce backstage. I hadn't quite expected the man I saw; he looked vile, like a reptile, with sins and sordidness etched in his prematurely lined face. He had sallow puffy features with what little hair he had brushed forward on his head in a vain attempt to cover his baldness. His hair was dyed black.

He wore a huge Siamese blue mohair overcoat, and, believe it or not, leather trousers over calf-length high-heeled chisel-toe boots. His shirt was pink with a black leather tie. He looked more fifty than the thirty-five the press reports said he was. I almost expected to see him carrying a teddy-bear, instead he was followed closely by an effete man whom he introduced as his secretary. This was the famous Royce, a man reputed to earn one thousand pounds *a day* through his songs and shows.

Royce was in rapture over my performance. "My dear Peter," he shrilled, "You've certainly found yourself a dish, a perfect dish." His eyes crept obscenely over me: I could feel myself blushing.

"We really must do something about this one, don't you think dear. I do believe that's a blush –oh, he's too too much. If I stay here a moment longer I shall certainly ravish him; he's a perfect pet. *Do* bring him up one night, and I'll write him a song. I can almost see it now. Love," he flapped his hands, "teenage love; my heart is pure just for you—I can see it now, you sweet thing."

He came over and patted my cheek like one of the old village women. I wanted to vomit, but was hypnotized into a blank stare by Royce's reputation meeting face to face in my mind with his real self.

After Royce had "gathered his skirts, and fled" as he himself said, I looked across at John. He was fuming.

"Dan, I don't know much about this business, but I know a damn sight more about life than you. You've just met up with a raving queer and he fancies you. Do you know what a queer is? You'd better get wise to them quickly otherwise you're going to get a nasty shock. You're a good looking boy, almost too good looking; they are going to think you're like them."

He paused. "But you know that. Go along with them part of the way if you think it will help your career, but I wish it didn't have to happen. I'd like to see you give up the whole idea and go back to Thickley rather than be corrupted by these sods."

John shouldn't have mentioned going back to Thickley. It rammed home to me the real reason why I had left—not just to play guitar, but to learn more about life and the world I lived in.

John misinterpreted the frown on my brow. "Promise me this, Dan," he said. "Promise me you'll never let them talk you into doing something you'll regret."

I looked at John. I couldn't grasp what he was saying. In a way he was implying that he himself had doubts about me. What was it with John ? Jealousy?

I shrugged my shoulders, dismissing the subject. It wasn't important anyway. I'd met one of the top men, and he liked my act. Not that I was keen on singing a Seymour Royce song, but I knew that with Royce's support, I could make the big time.

The following two weeks are engraved on my mind. They've crept into my nightmares of twitching and turning, again and again, not dulled by the screams nor blotted out by Mary's pills regularly rammed down my throat. It was during those two weeks that Peter Wickham-Smith began his slow seduction.

The terrible part is that I was just as much to blame as he was. I was young and very curious. Each minute of the day I would be brought face to face with my own limitations, lack of experience and knowledge, without the power to handle situations. I was so timid, at times I spoke almost in a whisper. If a booking clerk, for instance, didn't hear me when I asked for a ticket to Todworth, I'd almost throw a fit with the effort of repeating my request and drawing attention to myself. All this I wanted to cure.

In a way, I thought I recognized a kindred spirit in Peter. He was quiet, completely the reverse to Seymour, and seemed to be making a nervous effort every time he spoke or did something. I thought if I watched him he could perhaps help me.

So I came to enjoy the evenings we spent together. He told me Royce had flown to America for a few days but wanted to see me as soon as he came back. In the meantime, if I practised during the day he could take me around town in the evening introducing me to people who might be able to help. To me, this didn't seem a strange way of breaking into the business at all. I accepted it all as the normal procedure.

We met most evenings in the same pub I had first drunk in that night I went to the Two I's. Peter must have seen me in the pub that evening and kept a look out for me. The bastard!

"I suppose you are wondering why I'm so interested in you," he said one night.

I wasn't.

"I think it's because of my own past. When I was your age, teenagers didn't exist. All the people who had the good times were in their late twenties, it seemed. I've missed out on it all together, because now that I'm thirty, it's the teenagers' turn. I think if teenagers had been so important when I was your age, I'd have liked to be a singer too. Maybe that's what attracts me to you, makes me want to help you."

Gradually, his words and moves were getting bolder. We were talking about women once, at his instigation, and I told him about how I'd left Jill for the sake of my music.

"I've never had a girl friend at all," he told me, watching my face carefully to gauge my reaction. "I've never really liked women, frankly. I find them too insincere, weak, and repulsive. They are unnatural as well—all the make-up, they use. Ugh! I think you should bare your body unadorned and let the goodness in the air do the rest, don't you?

"Women aren't like that, though. Men are much better as friends, don't you feel? You can have a much more intimate relationship with a man, wouldn't you think?"

It was after a week of conversation on those lines that Peter decided the time had come to show me round. One evening he asked me if I'd like to go to a little club he belonged to.

"It's a very ordinary place, really. Just a bar and a few people. There's a juke box there, though, and there's bound to be some boys of your own age. You must be getting fed up with my company every evening, so it'll make a change for you."

As we climbed the stairs of this club—called after some Greek god; *Apollo*?—a fat bloke eased past us on the stairs, smiling lecherously at me. The club was in one of those back streets in Soho just off Shaftesbury Avenue, surrounded by delicatessens, Chinese and Italian restaurants, and contraceptive shops.

The entrance was an unimposing front door, rather like going up to someone's flat. I followed Peter dutifully into the club, a small room with about a dozen people. The proprietor, who looked like a wrestler, came over to us and made Peter sign my name in the visitors' book. He gave me an appreciative glance as Peter introduced me to him.

There were no women in the place, and I was aware of a dozen pair of eyes watching me as I went up to the counter. There was a horrible beery smell about the place and the cigarette fumes made my eyes smart. I had a fruit juice then turned to survey the other customers. There were three old men, around forty I suppose, chatting to young boys in jeans and bright sweaters.

There were a couple of Peter's friends in one corner and he took me over to introduce them. They were clerks at the Admiralty. Frankly, I didn't see the point of this place. If these were queers then they were a pretty unexciting lot. The boys looked like women, especially the two jiving together by the juke box. They'd certainly got all the mannerisms of women.

I was glad to leave. Next Peter took me across the road and down into a basement. This was a different place altogether. For a start there was a cloakroom attendant, a beaming proprietor, and three different bars. The place was luxuriously furnished, with a beautiful grand piano. A husky-voiced woman in a strapless evening gown was playing and singing popular melodies.

The bar customers were all dark-suited and very respectable looking. The boys looked as though they were on holiday from public schools and Peter said that neither women nor boys in jeans were allowed in except on Sundays which was a mixed-day. When I asked him about the woman at the piano, he told me she was really a man "in drag."

There were a few faces I vaguely recognized from seeing them on television and in the papers. Although people were obviously aware of me, they chose to ignore me, instead carrying on their conversations in low urgent voices. Peter took me over and introduced me to a middle-aged baronet wearing, what I was alter told, was an Eton tie. He bought me whisky, and said he was a director of a hot-dog machine, and wasn't that a great joke.

Peter explained to me that Sir Alan was really a very famous impresario. He put on many of Seymour Royce's shows. The conversation was a bit stiff, as it was obvious that Sir Alan and myself had nothing in common to talk about, and he couldn't really remember who Peter was.

As we walked from the bar, and I was beginning to feel a bit tight by now, Peter said: "Of course, you may have noticed that these people are queer, none of them like women at all. Did you recognize any people. You did? Some of them are quite famous. Did you see that man in the corner; he's a cabinet minister. You'll find that most of the really important people don't like women; they tend to sap one's strength if one's got ambition . . ."

I took it all in unquestioningly. I hadn't got the impetus to ask questions and it all seemed quite plausible anyway. We had come to a corner of Soho that I later discovered is the most popular place for the sort of coffee bar we were going into. At one time, it was a coffee bar opposite this one which was the favourite haunt of camp youngsters. That one got raided, and this one, Belle's, had opened. Now Belle's itself has been closed by the police and a new coffee bar has opened instead just round the corner.

Belle's was on the first floor over an ironmonger's shop. It was difficult to get in because of the crowd. There were boys and girls there but, for someone as green as me, the whole scene was utterly confusing. Many of those I took to be boys were actually girls, and lots of the girls turned out to be boys. And what amazed me is that they looked so normal and happy and young. There was a juke box on a stage and round it lots of people were jiving quietly. At the counter there were several older people watching the kids greedily, presumably sorting out whom they wanted for the night.

"You see, they're all kids like you here," Peter was saying. "They're having a fabulous time, without any inhibitions whatsoever. I wish I was a teenager now—you've got every opportunity to do exactly as you like with life, and no one is going to say no."

"No!" is what I should have said then. If I'd been a stronger person I should have walked right out of Peter's life and perhaps still be a little like I used to be. *But I didn't.* I stayed there not commenting, being fascinated by it all. Was it my silence Peter took as acceptance of his suggestions? Anyway, the next occasion worth recalling is a fateful party at Seymour Royce's flat a week or so later.

Seymour had come back from the States after negotiating a film deal for his 21st show. He wanted to celebrate and so threw a "Twenty-first birthday-party". "Come and help me reach maturity, dear," he said to Peter when he phoned him. "And bring that delicious new number of yours."

Seymour's flat was in Knightsbridge. It was the whole ground floor of a brand new block. He had his own basement garage where he kept his Rolls, a Mercedes, and a Bubble-car. The door to his flat was controlled by short-circuit TV with a microphone so he could see his callers.

Peter and I, very excited, went in to find ourselves in the most outrageous party—apart from orgies—I have ever been to. As soon as we entered, our coats were whisked away from us by a coloured boy dressed completely in white. Another boy (Danish, dressed in black silk) led us down the oak-panelled hall, lined with fruit-machines, into a huge lounge with, instead of a window, an enormous aquarium with all kinds of exotic fish gliding around. Hidden lighting gave the room an air of complete timelessness.

Seymour, radiant in a midnight-blue suit, was circulating round all the guests who included just about every top pop-singer in the business. I was knocked out! Another boy (Greek, red and white silk) handed me a glass brim full of brandy and champagne-punch. In my nervousness I drank it straight down, only to be given another one immediately. I stood uncertainly in the centre of the room whilst Peter was chatting to Seymour's secretary.

I was amazed by all these famous people—idols of mine whom I'd never accepted as being normal human beings—standing around chatting quite naturally to each other. They seemed unmoved by Seymour's frantic posturing and posing. Then he saw me. Greeting me with a shriek of delight, he came over with arms outstretched; I was frightened in case he was going to kiss me. I blushed.

Seymour was a fussy host, but a good one. He introduced me to all the singers and film stars. It astonished me to notice in the eyes of some of the singers that they probably had the same kind of thoughts and doubts about things that I had. But they weren't as embarrassed by Seymour as I was; they had known him a long time and it was mostly thanks to him that they had got anywhere at all. Being on edge, I drank more and more.

Every time I drained my glass another one was thrust at me. I just didn't know the potency of champagne and brandy and it wasn't long before I made my way to the toilet. Actually, I never got further than the beautifully furnished bathroom which had little steps up to a sunken bath in the centre of the room and a deep-piled carpet from wall to wall. There was even a Roman-styled couch. I've never seen so many gadgets and perfumes, which Royce seemed to think were essential to having a wash. But at that moment all I wanted to do was spew, which I did simply by collapsing on the steps to the bath and vomiting into it.

Fortunately for me, I have only very dim memories of the disaster which happened next. It was in the taxi that I regained consciousness slightly. My head was lolling on Peter's shoulder—I felt terrible. He half carried me up to his flat and laid me down on the settee. It was very late and, even if I were capable of catching it, I had missed the last train to Todworth.

Peter put some records on and started brewing coffee. For some reason, I wanted to dance. It was a flamenco record—all guitars and castanets—and I leapt up and started doing some really modern interpretive dancing. *Christ, I must have been high!* But so was Peter—he surprised me as I'd never seen him like that. I remember he danced with me, giving wild shouts of ole! He produced some whisky as well, which he proceeded to dose me with instead of the promised coffee.

Drinkwise, I did pretty well. I'm not so abandoned now, of course, when I get high, but it must have been an hour before I passed out again. All I remember of the next bit is something happening which I didn't like but didn't have the will to stop. I was just a lifeless and beautiful boy in a homosexual's flat.

When I woke up, it was seven o'clock. I was in a strange bed that I couldn't place at first. There was a man lying beside me; he had his arm stretched over my chest. We were both naked. On the floor by the bed was a jar of Vaseline. My body felt sore. I shuddered with horror.

The bastard.

CHAPTER 7

I didn't look any older. I mean, nothing showed about my face. It hadn't erupted in spots; there weren't even any shadows under my eyes. I may have lost a bit of suntan but that was inevitable as I wasn't on the farm every day. But I had always had the impression that the moment I started leading a debauched life, my physique and good looks would suffer.

My first reaction was obvious, of course. I realized that there wasn't really going to be a short-cut to success and the only way I would achieve anything would be to work at it. And that's what I did. With John and the bass-player, I began to play local dance halls and hops. John scoured every dance hall within a forty-mile radius to get us work. Once he realized how serious I was, he did his best.

I never told him what happened that night, but I could see that he was pleased I had severed my links with that crowd. The chance I may have thrown up by ignoring Seymour Royce (who did drop me a line asking me to call on him) seemed unimportant. I wasn't going to enter show business at that price. I realized that other singers had got into the business somehow and I was pretty sure sleeping with Seymour Royce and his associates wasn't the only way.

We began to get a lot of work within two short months. I'm not being immodest when I say that our act was good. My own subsequent success proves that, although when I look back it does strike me as a bit strong for us to have foisted the amateurism of my own style of music on teenagers and expected to get paid for it.

But we practiced hard. John and the bass-player kept their day time jobs and, fortunately, managed to stand the strain. They didn't play every night but I did. Soon I had a regular engagement playing in coffee bars, and a drinking club in Bushey, for three nights a week and then on Friday, Saturday, and Sunday I'd appear with the group. We billed ourselves as the Dan Gabriel Hot Three.

This leads me to my second reaction through Wickham-Smith. I will say this for him; he certainly made me pull myself together. I may still have looked like an innocent kid from the country but, boy, was I learning fast! It seemed obvious to me now that somewhere along the line sex was going to play a big part in this business. I'd seen pictures of pop stars going to film premieres with fabulous birds on their arms. If ever that should happen to me, I was determined to know the full score. If sex was going to play a big part then it was going to be normal sex pure and simple — and I was going to be good at it.

In a way, I must have gone about sex the way I went about playing the guitar. My dedication to sex became second only to my dedication to music. Of course, the process began slowly and it was ages before I developed the perfection I have now through so much practice! Actually, it wasn't that big an obsession with me—it was just that I had to have a woman to prove my masculinity, after Wickham-Smith. It all kind of snowballed from there, and my life, as I became a top singer, changed—in keeping with most teenage idols— into a relentless search for charver.

We used to borrow a van from a friend to get us to dance halls at weekends. This was ideal for carrying our guitars, amplifiers, and John's drums. Eventually, I planned to buy one but at this particular time it worked out cheaper to borrow. Our pay for the night usually covered the expense, although I had dipped into my savings to buy John additions to his drum-kit and on top of that I had to live off my evening earnings (which the other two didn't) so I was only just managing to scrape clear. I had no head for figures, and left all that to John. I would have liked him to give up work and look after me full time, but we decided to wait until we could by our own van on hire purchase before doing that.

The van we used to get to and from bookings became a regular knocking shop. We were playing Aylesbury, I think, and it was my second time out like this. We whipped up quite a storm for the show, and the kids loved it. There were some fabulous girls there with great lacquered bouffant hair-styles. I remember thinking how I'd like to crush one with my fist.

During the interval, I made for the bar. I got served without difficulty, which made a change because I still looked only sixteen. I saw one of these bouffant birds at the bar and offered her a drink. In her high heels she was about an inch or two taller than me, but what did I care.

I think it must have been then that I discovered something about the power of my eyes. Remember, I was still smarting over Wickham-Smith and was one-hundred-percent determined to get a girl, shag her, and then be on my way. This determination overcame my reserve, and really helped me to project myself through my eyes.

She was amused by a little tyke like me, with my flat Cheshire accent. My eyes seemed to embarrass her because I noticed she seemed to have difficulty in looking at me. When I saw her grow a shade pinker, even under all that make-up, I was like a new bloodhound; I wasn't certain what scent I was sniffing around for but this was it. She didn't take much chatting up, my playing had done that (another lesson) and I manoeuvred the conversation round to her waiting for me after the dance. She was chuffed!

The next move was simple. John and the bass player said they'd hang around for half an hour after the show and get a coffee. That would give me time.

I got the bird to help me carry the guitar to the van.

"How old are you, Dan?" she asked suspiciously. I guessed her friends had been ragging her. I turned the eyes on; she could see their deep sincerity in the moonlight. *What a knock-out!* I kissed her then without saying a word. This was going to be okay.

There was only a little difficulty getting her in the van. We had to open the doors to put the guitar in anyway, and another embrace resting on the back bumper, a quick shifty with the legs ("Hey, mind my nylons!") and she was in.

I closed the doors softly behind us, shutting out that ever-effective moonlight. Well, sex is the same anywhere, I suppose. I would have liked to take longer with the build-up but I only had half-an-hour. What if I'd picked a virgin, or a prick-teaser? I'd get even more twisted then. Fortunately I hadn't.

Now although I'm small, soft eyed, and beautiful, I'm what's known as donkey-rigged. There's no mistaking what's going on when I start. But I didn't know this then—I mean I didn't know this girl was enjoying it just as much as, in fact probably more than, I was. I thought I was using her. I was bloody nervous, of course, and wondered if I'd ever make it with a strange girl I'd never met until two hours before.

It was probably this tension in me which made it all the better for her. Stretched out between our guitar cases, equipment, a spare tyre, a tool box, and a drum kit, we were grinding away like Trojans; the springs of the Bedford van wheezing with happy protest as my little arse pounded up and down.

It was after we'd driven her home and were heading back to Todworth that the bass player congratulated me on my performance. He'd been watching through the back window. I didn't say much to him again.

Sometime during April, I left my Aunt's house and moved in with some friends on a houseboat. This was moored on the Grand Union Canal which ran right through Todworth. There were four of us living on the boat altogether; I shared a cabin with John. It was his idea that I should move in, and I liked it for the community feeling. Although I hadn't lived with anyone before. I did miss the comradeship of life in Thickley. I suppose I liked people to know what I was doing.

It's a funny thing, but my Aunt didn't even know her next door neighbour, so exclusive are people in the suburbs. Oh yes, the curtains were always flapping and gossip was rife, but there was no friendliness in Todworth like there was in Thickley. In this boat, with people of my own age, I came across a companionship and intimacy of living with people which I hadn't known before. If anything this only served to draw me out, although I was still regarded as being the baby of the outfit, a person who merited special attention.

We had parties there every weekend. John and myself used to arrive fairly late after we'd been playing a dance somewhere. We always brought some beer with us and occasionally a girl we'd picked up at the dance hall. I didn't like doing that though, because there was always the drag of having to get them home again on Sunday. But the Todworth talent wasn't too bad and already I'd become a fairly well known figure and reports had spread that I wasn't a refugee from the kindergarten after all but a virile hip-twitching rocker.

One Saturday night a new figure descended from the hatch. He was in his late twenties, a perfect picture of a wealthy self-made man in his grey hand-made overcoat with its velvet collar. He didn't seem anxious to attract attention, just walked over to where there was a row of glasses, pulled out a leather-bound flask from the depths of his coat, and carefully poured out a measure of whisky.

He handed this across to me and, as I disentangled myself from the bird I was snogging, I accepted it with a puzzled grin. He did the same to John who was also watching curiously. Then, he poured himself a drink form the same flask and started speaking. I'll always remember his first words.

"I'll not stay long," said the stranger, "as I'm aware that in this intoxicating atmosphere, anything I say will be regarded with the suspicion it would deserve were I also inebriated. I am not, however, and I have a proposition to make concerning your future, Dan, and yours as well, John. It is about your music, of course, and I would be obliged if you would do me the honour of joining me for dinner tomorrow. I am staying at the Station Hotel, a poor hostelry, I am afraid, but the best this abysmal town has to offer."

John was the sensible one, as always. I was just fascinated by the man's aristocratic accent. I thought he was a pompous idiot.

"What time," said John.

"I think one o'clock will be suitable, don't you."

"Okay, who shall we ask for?"

"Bernard Farrell. I'll look forward to seeing you." He drained his drink, climbed up the ladder and was gone.

The Sunday lunch passed pleasantly. The gist of the conversation was that the man was looking for a singer to invest some money in. He was strictly a businessman and, after studying pop music for some time, was convinced he had a formula which would guarantee good returns for his investment. He had also been studying the form of various singers and wondered if I would be interested in hearing his proposition. If I was, there was no need to even say so at the moment but visit him at his office in town at 9.30 a.m. the following day. He gave me a five pound note to cover fares.

Now I'd almost had this kind of chat before. But something about the man's arrogance and obvious professionalism made me think he could be accepted and even trusted. His card simply said The Farrell Group and gave a City address. Whatever it was he was after, the man had obviously gone to considerable trouble to seek me out. He brushed aside our questions in a very frustrating way, skilfully manoeuvring to get us to talk about ourselves. He seemed fairly knowledgeable about the film-business and asked John a lot of technical questions that impressed him.

The man said he knew Thickley, and Jill's father. This, of course, didn't make me any happier in view of the things I had been doing lately, but he assured me that Jill was well. She had just gone to Paris, he said, and would be spending a year in France. I suppose now that this was a calculated statement on his part but somehow my conscience became less irksome when I heard him say that.

The next day I was shown promptly into Mr. Farrell's office in a solicitor's suite in one of those big legal blocks near St. Paul's Cathedral. Mr. Farrell had apparently only just arrived, for he was just hanging up his overcoat as I walked in. He welcomed me with a smile which wasn't quite so arrogant, but nevertheless very businesslike. He motioned me to the seat at the opposite side of his desk. There was a telephone and a blotter on the desk, nothing else.

Mr. Farrell began by introducing himself properly. He had a number of businesses in the South of England, a record shop at Brighton, an amusement arcade somewhere else, and a string of coffee bars all along the South Coast. His main offices were in Brighton and he used these sparsely furnished rooms for any interviews he had.

"I am not a wealthy man," he told me, "but I'm a gambler. I have schemes, I find money to back them and if they turn out, I'm lucky. So far things have gone well; my failures have been set against my successes and I'm still head above water. But business, fascinating as it is, isn't entirely satisfactory to me.

"I am an artist at heart. I went to Brighton Art College and painting was to be my life, but then I inherited some money and decided to turn it to good use. The result is that my painting is a hobby and I find myself dealing with impersonal things for my daily wage. That's why I want to try this new venture; I want to create something artistic out of a human being.

"If that sounds vaguely sinister, it shouldn't. You will find me a very un-sinister man, utterly devoted to my work, women, and hobbies. Somewhat like you, I believe. But back to points.

"My record shop has given me an insight to the record business, as have the various cafes etc., which I've been associated with. It seems to me that, after the initial impact of the real raving rip-it-up-rocksters, pop music has reached a dismal stage of restrained rock-n-roll conservative style ballads. There's not the earthy spontaneity about pop music nowadays. Well, all this has got to change according to the swing of the pendulum. I estimate that it will change in about a year's time.

"Of course, many experts in the business would disagree with this. My own view is only based on a hunch. It doesn't matter if I'm wrong, as the kind of singer I have in mind should easily create his own demand. Are you with me?"

I nodded passively, wondering what was coming next.

"The spotlight of this modern world is on youth and that's fine, but such is the pace of life and the mediocre ability of many young people thrust to fame, that they don't last very long. Indeed, one has not only to have extraordinary talent but expert exploitation behind one, and the rare stature of a giant.

"There has been a series of teenage idols you have probably noticed who are gradually dying out. They are the `boy next door brigade'. Rock-n-roll has taken the star quality out of show-business in its frantic effort to prove that stardom can happen to anybody. In most cases it has and the results have been pathetic.

"Future star material, I believe, will have to be carefully moulded over the years. The new teenage idols will have to be so exceptional that, although they are from the same age group and appear to have a lot in common with their worshippers, they are in fact gods, no the boy next door.

"They can have opinions and expressions but only in keeping with a certain image. This image must bring them the respect of teenagers, the admiration of adults, and fantastic popularity with all record buyers and theatre goers. The singer will be a stand-no-nonsense, clear thinking, hard hitting young adult, at the same time being a mysterious nearly unobtainable idol.

"Where, you might ask, can a boy to fill this image be found? The answer is probably nowhere, but one can get very near to it. The rest is a matter of production technique. I have been searching for months and had almost given up hope until I heard about you. It was Seymour Royce who mentioned having seen you perform.

"But I'd like to make it clear that I am no admirer of Mr. Royce and his perversions. I have seen your act and think you have tremendous potential. You are, of course, incredibly raw but under my aegis I think we can create a boy who will fill most of my specifications and make us all a lot of money.

"I have checked up on you, discovered that you are patient and hard-working. This is good, because my plans for you are long-term and I don't want you to start despairing if things take longer than you expect, for I'm prepared to invest a fair amount of money and most of my spare time in your future."

It was all going way above my head now. I was far too excited to take much in. I had been watching Mr. Farrell occasionally scratch his crutch, tap his nose, or wave his finger at me to make a point. Never once did he touch the unopened packet of menthol cigarettes which he had thrown on his desk together with a leather-bound gas-lighter.

He was obsessed by what he was saying. This must have been the strangest interview a singer had ever had with a prospective manager. There was none of the artificial wooing behind the scenes, exploratory chats and shady propositions.

"The proposition I have to offer you is this. I will manage you as a singer. I am prepared to invest one thousand pounds to do this satisfactorily. I will mould you to a given image, which will be little more than a projection of your own exceptional personality.

"I will arrange for you to be produced as a pop artist; clothe you; pay your bills; provide you with pocket money: in short, I will look after your every need and whim until you start working. I will find you that work and then, when I do so, will take thirty per cent of your earnings, as well as of course, recovering any of that one thousand pounds I may spend in that period.

"Your work pattern, and to a certain extent your personal life, will be controlled by me. I don't intend to launch you into the big time straight away. It will be necessary to wait until both you and the public are ready. When they are, I will promote and advise you and be responsible for your welfare. You will find that you have to be a star twenty-four hours of the day. I will take any worries of behind the scenes work off your shoulders.

"Finally, before you start asking any questions, I must tell you what is in this for me. The main factor, of course, is money. I'll make no illusions about this. You are going to be in the £1,000 per week class. That means I'll be earning three hundred pounds a week from you. A very good investment, you'll agree. In actual fact, once various deductions, which I'll explain in detail later, have been made from the one thousand pounds, your own income will be around the same figure."

He paused wearily now, breaking open the cigarettes. He didn't offer me one. There was silence, I suppose he was waiting for me to speak. I tried to piece together what he had been saying, before breaking into a squeaky, "Well . . ." I was running my right thumbnail under the nails of my left hand, cleaning them nervously.

"You know where I come from. I'm a simple person. I don't know a thing about figures and motives." I looked at him carefully. His eyes returned my stare without flinching; he was a good man.

"John does; perhaps you could talk that over with him. I suppose he's my manager at the moment. But, yeah, I'm willing."

Bernard Farrell smiled at me; there was a surprising warmth in his face. "Yes, I want John to join us. In this business we'll need a road manager; John would like doing that. Anyway, all this can be boiled down into a contract. Your father will have to sign it as you're under twenty-one."

◆ ◆ ◆ ◆ ◆

Hey—I can't get over Mary, this nurse of mine. She's even a judo expert. Brown belt; that's good. She comes in whenever I want her like she's reading my thoughts; she taps my desires on the head before they get going. I'm like a child with her—the way she bullies me.

And, Christ!—how I hate her when she's holding me down when I'm having an attack. I don't get those so much now— they were just a kind of act really, like a spoilt brat. I think she knows it, too. Maybe all alcoholics are like that.

◆ ◆ ◆ ◆ ◆

The next few weeks rushed by. Dad came down to London and signed the contract, and I got down to work. Under this arrangement, I seemed to be working harder than I'd ever worked on the farm.

Mr. Farrell, as I called him until much later, had a flat at Hyde Park Gate as well as a house just outside Brighton. As he rarely used the flat and wanted us in London all the time, he made John and myself move in. John didn't want much persuasion to come and work full time with me; he doted on me, and I'm afraid later I took advantage of him.

I was very much dependent on him to sort me out, get me to appointments on time (I always seemed to get lost in the Underground) and speak to people (I was becoming completely wrapped up in what I was learning and would go without talking, or eating, for hours).

Philip Le Tissier, the top freelance television producer had been engaged by Mr. Farrell to begin what he described as the "image making".

He found a bass player, Jimmy Parker, who later joined me permanently for nearly a year, and hired a rehearsal room to hear my act. Jimmy was older than us and a professional musician. He knew most of the numbers I did, and soon picked up the few I had written myself. He didn't speak much but kept to himself, regarding this as just another gig.

Jimmy went home after Mr. Le Tissier had heard us playing for about two hours. I have never felt so flat in my life as I did then. That producer, though, had worked out which were my strong points, and began to devise an act.

He came to the flat each day, putting me through my paces, while he made John practice better flexibility on the drums.

"The audiences at big stage shows are mostly girls in the thirteen to eighteen age group," he said. "A singer's appeal to them can be varied. He can be a straight beauty ballad type singer. Then more in the teenage vein, you can have the baby-faced sex bomb capable of doing a few excitable turns or coping with a slow love number. Then there's the wild ravers who beat the guts out of a piano, strip off their jackets and shirts, and leap all over the stage. Maybe they get one or two hit records, but they don't last.

"There are offbeat striking-looking singers with an earthy haggard kind of appeal; the same as looking sexy. They look like they want to be mothered. I think that's probably the nearest to you. Of course, there are those lads who writhe with every beat and practically copulate with the microphone on stage, but I don't think that would suit your personality at all.

"With you, your natural ingenious charm and reserved way off stage can be both a hindrance as well as a help to your image. Obviously we are going to have to build you up similar to what you actually are; a good looking country lad. Whether you're allowed to have girl friends and drinks, I don't know yet, but your act has got to carry something more than good looks and simplicity. At the moment you just stand still without moving much. You've got to project yourself much more than that.

"There is a slight movement of your legs which you can develop more, a kind of trotting on the spot. And I think the odd prowl round the stage would be very good. Another excellent way of exciting a young audience, particularly in your case with you looking so desirable to everyone out there, is to sing with someone.

"Maybe we could work out something with John. If you were to put your arm on his shoulder, not round it completely, that's much too camp, just kind of resting on him, that would go down a bomb. It brings you into contact with someone, you see. Your audience have an identification point.

"Timing is very important in all this. There must be thought behind every gesture. Yours is going to be the little-boy-lost-and-all-alone-and-searching-for-someone-to-love-and-its-you-you-you appeal. You mustn't look vicious on stage at all, no kicking or wild prancing. Everything must be controlled. The lighting of course will help pinpoint your isolation. Single spotlights, etc. We'll work out a standard lighting plan for each of your numbers.

"We'll have to choose those numbers correctly as well. Of course, this is just for stage work where you've got a captive audience all duty bound to watch you. In dance halls it will be different. You'll have to project yourself more, but not so much that you compete with the dancing, because that's what you are there for, to provide music rather than a hero-figure. We'll have to keep everything clean as well; there's to be no sex in this act, I've decided. You're just not capable."

I listened to these lectures each day completely fascinated.

I watched a new creature I barely recognized grow up. They said they were merely projecting myself into an image every girl could grasp. I didn't see it.

"It's a good thing being small," Philip said one day, "Girls will feel protective towards you. Don't worry about that. Your singing is hard, though; it's got guts. So boys will go for you too. I doubt if many of them are bent, but you'll seem an inoffensive idol for their girl friends to have, so they won't mind.

"It's good to turn your back on the audience occasionally as well, just to keep everyone happy. Later on we'll have to take the guitar from you—it'll give you more chance to project. You can keep it for a while though.

"You are simple and you're clean and you've got a kind of winsomeness. You're out on stage for a fantastic rave —but not a sexual one."

My name presented a problem for a while. One evening, Farrell and Le Tissier dropped in and he and John had a long discussion about what I should be called. We waded through such names as Saul Lust, Norman Passion, Dan Satan, Rummy Duggan, Dan de Lion (ouch!) Toby Jug, Mark Venus. It's amazing how silly you get trying to think of a name. Le Tissier did a re-cap.

"Now get this. He's a sweet innocent farm lad whom the girls want to protect, he's lovable; cheery and above all clean in his act; he's a kid; doesn't even shave yet; he's small; he's got blond hair; brown eyes; he's fresh, invigorating, exciting, he reeks of the country, well perhaps not quite like that; his first name is Dan. That's good, strong and got impact. Now we want another name that fits in, captures a wholesome countryside with a bit of glamour about it."

"Straw," said John.

"Think of the weather," said Bernard.

"Nasty" said John, "Or how about Damp ?"

"You're a lot of help," said Le Tissier, "we might as well call him Dan Stairs if you're going to be like that. Or Dan Tools—his father was a shop steward at Fords."

It was when they had got round to Dan Turpin, that I suggested that since they thought I was angelic, why not Angel Gabriel. They all stared at me in amazement.

"Gabriel's cute," said Algernon. "It says soooo much."

"But not Angel, for God's sake," said Le Tissier. "I'll throw up."

"OK," I said. "Why not Danny Gabriel?"

They seemed amazed at *Danny* Gabriel because people always called me Dan—on account of Dan Archer, I suppose. But that was it. Henceforth I became Danny Gabriel. The next few nights were spent practising my autograph.

Although I was satisfied at the instruction I was getting, I was anxious to start putting it into practice. Bernard realized this, and managed to get me a late booking for the summer season in Jersey.

I was on my way.

CHAPTER 8

Jersey is the worst possible place Bernard Farrell could have chosen for me to spend the summer. Sure, it's a fabulous little island with its quaint system of government and police state, its proximity to France, and the beautifully relaxed atmosphere. It's the relaxed atmosphere with its correspondingly relaxed morals that finally got me. But we weren't to know that would happen as we set out from Gatwick airport on a Jersey Airlines plane.

The hotel I was booked to play in had a fair size bar open to non-residents, and we were told it was one of the most popular on the island for young people. We had been booked to play from 8 p.m. till 11 p.m. each evening, except Mondays. We would be there for eighteen weeks and I would be earning sixty pounds per week.

But Bernard had plans for the sixty pounds, which I hadn't anticipated. For a start there was his percentage to come off which reduced my pay to forty two pounds. From this I had to pay John and Jimmy, and put some by as a tax reserve. That meant the two boys were getting twelve pounds each and I, as the singer and lead guitarist, was getting fifteen pounds. At the time, it didn't seem too bad for eighteen hours work a week but then it hadn't occurred to me that in a small island like Jersey, as all over England for me now, my private life wasn't private and I had to keep up my image all the time.

For young people Jersey was (and still is) important for two things: sex and drink. It seemed ironical that these should be the two distractions that were in danger of plaguing my guitar playing. I was like all newcomers to the island at first; fairly subdued as I looked around me in amazement. As I was working in the evenings, I didn't have an opportunity to join in the nightly raves they had at different pubs either in town or on the coast.

The first few days were spent in final rehearsals, a press interview and general preparation. Mr. Farrell had ordered some stage-suits for us and these didn't arrive until the day before our opening. Mine was made of a light-grey material, a combination of mohair and wool. Mr. Farrell considered this more practical than something like Italian silk, which, although it looked good, tended to crease very easily. I was pleased to find that the tailor, who made suits for practically all the stars, had added a small pocket behind the lapel. This was for a spare plectrum, should I suddenly lose one while playing on stage.

Our opening was a tremendous success. It would be a lie to say I wasn't nervous before we went on stage. I was, but I was also strangely confident. I had implicit faith in both Bernard Farrell and Philip Le Tissier. I tended to give people I trusted my whole soul and with these two I had gone all out to do exactly what they said, so convinced was I that they were right.

The ovation which greeted me at the end of the evening, after we had sweated through every number we knew to fill out the time, was astonishing. As it was a bar with people drinking all the time, our presentation had been more relaxed than with stage work. But we had created a sensation. Mr. Farrell was satisfied.

After that first night, I tended to regard this stint as a necessary apprenticeship to the greater things promised. I enjoyed every minute of it, though, even if I did wonder at times about losing my spontaneity through playing the same numbers night after night. The odd whisky, I found was a help here. That all began on our first evening off.

Mr. Farrell had gone back to the mainland and so John and myself were left alone. He had given me a lecture before he went about the importance of this work, but he didn't mention the dangers of deviating from the perfect character he had moulded for me. Why should he, when he thought there were no flaws to my personality? To a certain extent, apart from the lapses when I was finding my feet, there weren't any. I was blissfully happy now, without a thought for anything but being a success.

I don't know why I took to drinking but I suppose it was

generally to relieve the stagnancy of my act. Of course, we changed it around as much as we could but even for someone who loved playing as much as I did, this did represent a strain which drinking helped to brighten, also I had ample opportunity being in a bar, especially as so many people wanted to buy me drinks. I didn't drink much during the day, though, but—after getting up around noon—spent my time in the sun or, if it was raining, in the cinema.

I spent hours in the sun on the beach and joined all the beach games I could, and swam a lot. As can be imagined, I was becoming an even finer physical specimen than when I was on the farm. The sea and the sun bleached my hair slightly, and my body took on a glorious sun tan and attracted many an admiring gaze from the birds and blokes on the beach.

A little personal fan club sprang up for me, and each night a team of people I had played on the beach with, would turn up at the hotel. They sat round tables in front of the stage, patiently watching every movement, clapping wildly at the end of each number. Other customers, mostly flash fast-talking holiday makers from London drank flamboyantly. I was shrewd enough to keep my drinking a secret. I kept a rum bottle in a guitar case and if I found I wasn't getting enough drinks sent up from the bar, I'd have a quick swig in the dressing room when no one was around.

Of course, people noticed how I opened up a bit with drink but they put it down to the music. Many girls used to come along and, for the first month or so, I took no notice of them. I didn't need them now. This only attracted them more because, being so good looking and innocent, I was a challenge to their femininity.

None of them succeeded, however, until one night in June. I went back to my room a bit more stoned than usual. I was feeling gloriously happy. John had stayed in the bar where he was chatting one of the waitresses. That suited me fine.

I stumbled up the stairs and opened my door. There was a girl in my bed, fast asleep. Now what normal boy wouldn't have done what I did? Although John's bed was empty and I could have easily got in that, this situation intrigued me. There was nothing in my contract, after all, that I shouldn't sleep with women. I didn't know her but she looked quite pretty. I stripped off and climbed in beside her.

That night was the most glorious sex I'd ever had. I'm not kidding, it was *fabulous!* This was the first time I had spent a whole night in bed with a girl and I made the most of every moment. If she was one of the Jersey slags I had heard so much about, then I wanted more of them. You can picture it, can't you? It was a summer's night and we were both like little sun children. She had white streaks of flesh across her breasts and thighs, which made her more desirable.

So the season dragged on, each evening becoming more and more hectic, and my drinking getting worse and me getting happier. I had become so popular in the bar that I was transferred to the ballroom. But this didn't alter things.

Every night the same thing used to happen. I'd get drunk . . . and when I got drunk I started to behave completely out of character to my normal self. Any girls who came into my dressing-room I used to grab. I was under the impression when I was drunk that once I kissed a girl she would be mine for the night.

But there was still enough of Dan Glover in me not to do anything without suitable encouragement. If a girl jokingly said something about how sweet I looked on stage and she wondered what it was like to go to bed with an angel—as those girls often did—my senses would flare up and that woman wouldn't stand a chance.

I was convinced I was the world's best lover and wondered how anybody could resist me (*I still am!*). It so happened that this approach worked every time. Each night, it seemed, I stumbled back to my room with a bird. Once we were in bed I was completely shattered and used to pass out. But when I woke up in the morning with a strange girl I couldn't remember having got there, I really made up for it. *Boy! How I went to town!*

Was it inevitable that I should move in with a girl instead of whoring around all the time? I don't think so, but it happened. Maureen was a nude model from London who worked in the hotel as a barmaid, and she took me in hand. Like me, she was free during the day, and spent the time sunbathing in the nude on the roof of her flat. It wasn't just working hours I'd got in common with her: she liked rum.

In fact it was Maureen who started me on rum as soon as I woke up. She drank it like medicine. So desperate was she for sun that she'd leap out of bed about eight, knock back some rum straight from the bottle to revive her, and then go up to the roof and stretch out in the sun all day. Occasionally she would go into the kitchen and fix herself a salad or something, or a lager from the fridge. I soon fitted in with her routine, drinking during the day to kill my boredom at lying around doing nothing, and drinking at night to relieve the strain of doing the same act to the same crowds of people all the time. I was getting into a terrible state.

John watched what was going on for a while. If I hadn't moved out of the hotel, he probably wouldn't have said anything, but when he realized I was escaping from him and beginning to depend on someone else, he got wild.

Maybe it was through jealousy rather than real concern for my welfare that prompted him to phone Mr. Farrell and tell him the score. Anyway I'm not even sure that I'm grateful that he did. If he'd let things lie I would probably have just drifted out of the business without too much damage being done. As it was, the final showdown was postponed. Bernard Farrell came over and read the riot act. I remember being hauled before him in his hotel room early in the morning he arrived. I wasn't sober, and my breath reeked of rum. He looked at me and sneered disgustedly.

"I don't understand it, Danny. You look just the same. From what I hear you've been leading a life to put Dorian Grey to shame. What are you trying to do to us? We've got a great future ahead; you must realize that I'm not going to have this jeopardized by your drinking and trolling around

"I realize it was probably my fault in expecting too much of you too soon. You obviously don't understand what is at stake. You've got it in you to be not only a top star, a top money maker, but a guitarist and singer everyone will look up to. You are an ordinary farm labourer from Thickley who can make the big time. What about your natural sense of proportion and responsibility? Has that all vanished in the phoney bum's life you've been leading? That's not the real Dan Gabriel, and you know it."

John just said that he came in for a reprimand for not watching me carefully, I was moved back to the hotel and John was instructed to help me cut down on the drinking. It wasn't easy, of course, to suddenly halt the dissolute and enjoyable life I'd been leading. There had to be something in its place.

Of all the influences, it was John's affection for me which pulled me through then. He loved me, and was determined that I should succeed. Now his course had been set for him his determination was infectious. We spent our spare time until the end of the season plotting my future, song writing, even—this was John's idea and a clever one—exploring the countryside. I kept away from the destitutes, the deadbeats, of Jersey and the little clique at St. Brelades. The result was that I flew back to London at the end of the season a wiser man, ready as ever I would be for the big time.

CHAPTER 9

You know, in London, thousands of people seem to be rushing in one direction for no particular reason, at the same time as thousands of people are rushing back from that direction. It would seem to be a sensible idea for someone to call a great conference and sort people out. The only time I've ever seen people smile in the streets of London is when they come across a busker playing in the gutter. Watch their eyes light up as a little bit of joy penetrates their haggard minds.

I think the government should employ street musicians to play outside all busy underground stations and queues. People would feel a lot better for it and they wouldn't have to cross over the road to avoid beggars. Payment could come out of rates and taxes. Maybe I'll become a busker when I get out of here!

I started a hectic schedule. Bernard had decided that I ought to get used to appearing at different towns and dance halls every evening. This was similar to what I had been doing at Todworth and Thickley but on a much larger scale. We had more travelling to do, often going into East Anglia or down to Southampton, or even on a few occasions up to the Midlands.

Bernard bought us a van to cut down on fares and carry our gear. If ever we were too far away from London to get back for the night, we used to unroll our sleeping bags and kip in the back of the van. He got all those bookings through acquaintances, or through promoters in those particular areas. As word about our act spread, there was no shortage of work.

These fringe groups, as Bernard called them, could earn a fair wage each week. Local promoters, more for improving their own finances than for providing somewhere for youngsters to go, hired a hall, a "bouncer" and a band—well, a group like ours. They then sat back and raked in the takings. It didn't matter about us not being well known. The kids went to the dance halls for any fringe singer; in a way we served as substitutes for their unobtainable real idols.

Fringe groups were (and still are) big business. For every singer on disc, there were probably twenty fringe groups all working reasonably hard. Some of them were part-time popsters but that's a strain, for there's not much going to bed early. After a while, a fringe singer gets a regular circuit, like I did, and a regular and growing crowd of fans.

Unfortunately although we were happy working like that, everything in the fringe was not lovely. There are some ruthless and very crooked people in the business. Some are the characters who set themselves up as managers and then get a booking for a group for £40 a night but only pay the group £15. That's an old dodge.

At one of the shows I did, the organizer said he would send my money on to Bernard the next day. It never arrived. When we tried to get in touch with the fellow, he'd moved on. After that if the promoter wasn't known to us, John, who had by now given up drums to manage me exclusively, would stand at the box office each evening until the money had been collected and handed over.

On another occasion, I was billed to appear at a town I had often visited. I had a good following there, but when the dance started only a few people turned up. John looking round the town to see what had happened, discovered cancelled notices had been pasted all over the posters. New posters had been stuck up advertising a dance run by a rival promoter at the same time at another hall.

The biggest fiddle I came across is what you might call white-guitarist traffic. A few shrewd operators, working independently but all with the same approach, used to tour dance halls where local groups played for cheap. Using a lot of spiel about their connections with the big stars, these operators would offer the group a chance of a full time engagement abroad if they were interested.

Of course the lads in the group, probably factory workers by day, would jump at the chance. The operators, setting themselves up as managers, would offer the group a low percentage contract, and arrange them a season booking at continental clubs (Germany and France were favourites), or at American bases in Europe.

The manager would probably drive them over to the continent in his own van, see them settled in, then come back to find some more unsuspecting part-time popsters. He made his cut by paying the groups fifteen pounds per week each instead of the twenty-five pounds per man that he received for them.

Of course, sometimes a group would find out what was going on, in which case the manager would abandon all knowledge of them and they would have to sort themselves out. To safeguard their own interests, as well as those of the groups they employ, foreign promoters have begun to insist on dealing only through a recognized booking agent, instead of direct through a group's manager. Even so, with the passing of a few perks here and there, the racket is still going on.

For what I got from Bernard, I think I had a good arrangement; he was taking a high cut but gave me a lot for it. It seems to me that the only people who make the money consistently out of the teenage section of show business, are the percent men.

Satisfied by the reaction I provoked and the way my personality and act was shaping, Bernard decided the time was ripe for the next section of his plan to be put into operation. I had been working then without any publicity, getting sufficient work by reputation alone.

Bernard had plans for a record. It was coming up for Christmas then and none of the recording companies wanted to know. Bernard decided that their interest might be greater if my name was mentioned in the press a few times. Then, together with a demo disc I would make for him at his expense, he would have some ammunition.

The man Bernard chose to do my publicity was a real dynamo, dashing away to conversations on telephones while he talked to us at his flat where he had converted one room into an office. The walls of his lounge were covered with plaster friezes copies from ancient ones in the British Museum.

His bedroom had something I had heard about but never actually seen—a two way mirror. The door from the lounge into his bedroom looked as though it had an ordinary mirror set into it, but from the other side it was just like a window.

This publicist used to watch his friends performing when he put anyone up for the night. The most decorated room in the flat was his toilet. Every square inch was papered with pin up poses of idols.

"I can get you all the publicity in the world," he told me and Bernard, "but we've got to work along the right lines and be consistent. There's no good in me starting something now and then abandoning it next month. For one thing, the teenage magazines work weeks in advance. I'm glad you've come to me now—so many aspiring popsters come in here saying they've got a record out next week and could I do something about it. All I can do is to tell them to get stuffed—it's much too late then.

"I can start by getting you in the girls' magazines, gradually building up national interest in you as a person. Soon people will start inquiring about you and your records. By that time, you should have a record out.

"I can also get you teeny mentions in the musical papers which lets those in the trade know that you're around. Then, if we can think of something really good, we can break a story in the nationals. This would be best about record release time so that we have a definite title to plug.

"It's all very well saying fans rioted at Slosgam dance hall and fifteen hundred people were arrested. That might get you a headline, but it won't do you any good. It won't sell anything if you've got nothing to sell.

"When your record comes out, it'll be my job to get it reviewed. There are around three dozen new singles each week. Obviously not all of them are going to get a mention. To get a mention in the nationals is the ultimate, especially a favourable one. People will look out for your disc and, if they hear it on the radio and they like it, you're made.

"Of course, once you do get your feet off the ground the magazines and papers will be coming to you automatically. My job is simpler then, as they'll come up with a lot of the ideas. Newsworthy things will happen to you.

"You have to react in keeping with your image, though. Then—to keep you automatically constantly before the public eye—I have to think of even bigger ideas, just to keep the show ball rolling.

"The next stage is to take some notice of an old dictum they teach every new reporter. The people who make the news are those who want to keep out of it. So we shut up on you, don't release a thing; do a Garbo almost. When that happens and it works, you know you're at the top.

"To get you in the fan magazines, we start coupling you with other singers, say something like 'In his spare time, Adam Faith likes watching Danny Gabriel at the local Palais'. A few mentions and the girls will want a photo of you. Then we start bringing your name in on a problem page, featuring the views of the big names, with your view squeezed in the middle.

"Then we could fly you to the States but only in press releases, of course, not really. We could have Elvis Presley saying what a great guy you are, or Brenda Lee saying you're divine. It's all right, the big American names won't know if they've met you or not, and the British names won't mind being mentioned, especially if I'm handling their publicity as well.

"For the trade paper titbits we'll try to have you photographed escorting a big name like Alma Cogan to a film premiere. Alma's a marvellous girl, she'll willingly help a newcomer all she can.

"National paper stories are different. We can always have a policeman forbidding his daughter to have anything to do with you, that's favourite. But maybe that's not your image. We've got to get across how good you are, that's not so easy.

"Record reviewing is where my own personal contacts come in. I'll breathe the word around about your disc when it comes out. I'll chat up disc-jockeys and columnists. You know, I have to keep up with people who are complete drags just because they can help with the protege of the moment.

"I'll need pictures galore to illustrate copy. All sorts of poses.

"Then when you get really big—and I'm sure you will— you might find it a good thing not to be photographed too often. For your image, make sure you are never photographed with a girl, unless it's a top star or you're signing a fan's autograph. You'll have to be careful like that."

Bernard paid him forty guineas to create interest in me up until the time my first disc was released, and then he was to receive eight guineas weekly to promote me for the next three months. We'd then review the situation.

The publicist did fairly well, although the write ups never appeared in anything I used to read. Bernard used to show me cuttings from strange magazines like *My Man* or *Woman's Monthly*, which mentioned me. One write-up had me throwing a red-pepper-risotto-party at my luxury flat and ended up: "A natty note I spotted in Danny's bedroom. He has hung a huge fisherman's net complete with cork floats, on one whitewashed wall. It sprawls most effectively looks good with raffia shades and woven rugs. Gives a room terrific personality." I ask you!

When that appeared I had entered into another big romance. I met Jan at the time of my 19th birthday. Someone in Notting Hill was giving a party on that same day, so I went along with John to this basement. The party itself was a riot with the scum of the London drinking clubs very much in evidence.

The host was serving a delicious and very potent punch. Its potency was obviously an unknown quantity for it wasn't long before the whole party was drunk—some having a bit of sex-fun, some fighting according to how drink affected them. It made me bolder than usual so when I saw this girl with close-cropped hair contemplating me from the door, I walked over. She reckoned she was bored as well, and said why didn't I go to her flat around the corner for coffee. I did, stayed that night, and began a remarkable relationship.

Jan was a lesbian. I know I'm always getting caught up with the kinky ones, but that's just how life was to me. She was what they call "butch", the type of girl who has to boss any situation. After having my life jealously run by John and the experience I'd had with women in Jersey, Jan was a fascinating contrast.

John met her, of course, and saw the dingy little room I had moved into with her. When he saw that I wasn't having sex with Jan, he must have decided the relationship was only temporary and wouldn't do much harm. Bernard was away in America on a three week business tour, so we couldn't ask his views. I was still playing practically every evening and it seemed to me that I ought to be allowed to live where I chose, providing I kept it all to myself.

Why Jan liked me being with her, I don't know. I was sufficiently masculine and matured to make damn sure she didn't try any of her butch ways or kinky sex with me. I reckoned she was just a very lonely girl, and it was a change for her to have someone who liked her as a person instead of as a brief affair. We slept together, had cuddles, but as soon as I started getting roused Jan would switch of the sweetness, tell me not to be naughty and settle down to sleep.

I suppose this seems frustrating (it does to me now, I'm just panting for a hump) but over the weeks I developed a peace of mind—a bit like married couples who are past it —which outshone any sexual satisfaction.

My day was full. Maybe they should give me some occupational therapy now instead of those damn pills. I started having image lessons. Philip Le Tissier and the publicist, Algernon Keen, did all but make me strip in front of them. One would make me talk while the other watched my mannerisms. They took me out to dinner and talked social nonsense to see how I reacted, which knives and forks I used, what I knew about ordering.

They took me to the theatre and the cinema. They even roped Jan in so that they could observe how I behaved with women in public. Gradually they built up a composite picture of the real Dan Gabriel. Now they began the task of transforming me into the Danny Gabriel they wanted the fans to know.

To fit in with my wholesome image, it was decided that I wouldn't smoke (I didn't) nor drink (I did). In future, in public it was to be cokes. I was to like pure health foods and homemade goodies such as apple pies. They wanted to preserve a country-bumpkin air about me.

Little mannerisms of mine, such as my enquiring glances, they developed. They taught me how to use my eyes to the full extent, holding them on other people longer than normal. They worked on my accent which was becoming Londonised and replaced the slang expressions I had picked up, with country-sounding phrases.

They told me the sort of clothes I was to wear, white on stage but my daily clothes were to have a simple country gaucheness about them. I was always to be sun tanned, so a sun-ray lamp was bought for regular sessions. I was to have no sex life at all, wasn't to swear, make profound statements (or any statements, come to that) and was to have an ingenuous appearance.

So while I personally was becoming more sophisticated, my image as a singer was reverting to the churlish boy I had been a couple of years previously in Thickley. It was very confusing.

Bernard came back from the States in a good mood, his business had gone well and he was convinced he had found the new sound he was looking for. He said that this particular music was very big over there, and was bound to create a smash in England. Called "The Rave" it was ideal for me not only because the dance suited my stage act, but also because the lyrics were good clean entertainment.

So as to be the first with it in England, he worked on some new lyrics to a rave rhythm, which I recorded on a demo disc. Bernard hawked this around the studios but without success.

When he heard that I was living with Jan, Bernard hadn't protested as much as I had expected. He saw that Jan was having a good effect on me and, probably fearing that I'd start drinking in a big way again if he stopped our friendship, turned a blind eye to it. I wasn't a big star, after all, and we were being very discreet about our relationship. I was drinking quite a lot; my capacity had increased, and I found I couldn't do without a few whiskies or brandies every day.

One evening, towards the end of March, Jan and myself went to a Lesbian drinking club in Notting Hill Gate. People were only admitted if personally known to the manager. A couple of girls who had been going together for a few months were being married that evening. It was a bizarre affair, with an old Catholic priest, who had been unfrocked for interfering with choir boys, performing the ceremony. This followed the standard church service except that the groom was a girl looking surprisingly pompous in hired tails and a top hat. The bride wore white.

There was a reception afterwards, and we all got rather tight. One girl, in fact, decided to renew an old feud she had with Jan, and it wasn't long before her hatred of Jan (and perhaps, of her happiness with me) flared into violence. The girl quite suddenly grabbed a beer mug and tipped the contents over Jan's hair. Then she started thumping the mug on her head.

Jan and myself, both pissed, didn't realise what was happening. The smashing of the glass against the door and seeing this girl lunging at Jan with the jagged edge brought me to my senses. I grabbed her and with the help of some of the girls, overpowered her. That's the only time I have ever fought with a lesbian; they are real Amazons when they get going.

We were in bed when she started sobbing. It was dreadful. A great cloud of despair settled on her, and she clung to me howling at the lonely emptiness she had to live through being queer. After an hour, she stopped, lying quietly cradled in my arm.

She was a new person. I leaned over and kissed her softly. Her lips accepted mine, then, as I lifted my head, clung to me ferociously. Clawing and raging, we tore at each other in fierce and demanding lust. We fell apart exhausted as the spurts of love subsided.

Suddenly Jan shrieked, pounding my body with her fists, pushing me away from her.

"Get out ! Get out !"

I thought she was having a fit, and snapped on the bed-side light. "Get out, get out" she kept on shouting.

She leapt out of bed, her naked body throwing weird shadows on the wall from the light. She ripped the blankets off me, grabbed my arm and hauled me to the floor. "Get out, get out."

Now that's no way to treat a man just after he's come his lot. I ducked to avoid a cigarette box as it whistled past my ear. That was followed by my clothes, an ashtray, three books, a couple of LP's and then the alarm clock.

She calmed down eventually, I talked softly, very nervous, wondering what had gone wrong. "All right," I said, "I'll go. But not now, it's too late to go anywhere."

"Now—I don't want you in bed with me any more."

"Okay, I'll sleep on the floor, then. I'll make a bed up here and leave first thing in the morning." I put her back into her own bed. She fell asleep whimpering.

The following morning, Jan was true to her word. She refused to talk about the previous night. My affection for her changed to hatred. If she wanted me out that was all right by me. I didn't need her. What's more, I wouldn't come back even if she begged me to. I didn't say a word as I dressed and packed my grip, neither did she.

There was only one place to go, and that was Todworth. My pride had been hurt and I needed time off to work out why. It so happened that I didn't get much chance to brood. In the carriage of the train I caught at Baker Street was a lonely old duffer, a typical retired-colonel type with his bloated red face, brisk clipped white moustache and blue regimental tie.

We got chatting and when I told him I was a singer he was tremendously impressed. He asked me if I was appearing anywhere that evening. I wasn't. After a few more questions about my act, he asked if I'd care to appear at a ball he was organising that same evening in aid of spastics. It was being held at his country estate a few miles beyond Amersham.

"I can't pay you, old boy, as it's for charity. I'd be dashed grateful if you'd do it. Billy Fury was to have come but Larry Parnes says he's been taken ill." The old boy shook his head as though he didn't believe it.

It was the Princess being there which caught us all off guard. In fact, I hadn't even told Bernard about the engagement, so one can't really blame him for not being prepared. When I went on stage with the boys, there were all these deb types gawping at each other and stiffly trying to rock to the lifeless music of some stuffed-shirt professional dance-band. We took over, and after the initial hush, proceeded to rip up the place. But it wasn't until I introduced my new dance, the Rave, to them that things went berserk.

I did some of the numbers Bernard had brought from the States and then, when the audience had got used to my music, demonstrated how to dance the Rave. I just grabbed the nearest girl and started raving. I noticed the other dancers were watching astonished, but honestly didn't realise why. This girl was raving fit to bust, and everybody was having a ball. It was four in the morning when she left.

I remember a bloke asking me my name, camera flashes popping, and then I must have slumped into semi-consciousness. I was pretty cut up with the day's drinking. John took me home to Todworth, none of us aware of the pandemonium about to break out.

CHAPTER 10

There was a time when I felt so happy, so good-looking, so wonderful to be alive. I couldn't move without being mobbed, and it wasn't just the Hairies or Uglies who chased me, it was everyone. Everyone wanted my jissom.

Now I'm here, all alone. I curl up, fondle my gristle, and wait for the drugs to slow down my mind and make me relax. I suppose I'm getting better now—it's been long enough. I don't shriek so much, fidget so much, or even crave so much. I'm just here, recovering by degrees, wondering what it's going to be like when I get out; remembering what it was like before I came in.

The first morning in Todworth; the hissing voice, the bright light when I wanted to sleep.

"Dan," my aunt was hissing urgently, "wake up, dear. There're some people here to see you."

People? People? What did people want with me at that time? What sort of people barged into a man's bedroom when he's only just gone to bed? What sort of people didn't give a man a chance to sleep off the effects of champagne and a Spastics Ball?

"They're journalists, Danny. They want a word with you," my aunt said again, with more firmness.

I opened my eyes cautiously. For a moment I thought I had woke up in the booking-hall of Piccadilly Underground station.

Grouped around my bed were a dozen people. It was a small room, with the wardrobe and dresser in, there wasn't much space for anything apart from me and the bed. But these reporters had managed it. I blinked, not so much because of disbelief, but because of the flash bulbs exploding all over the place. The lessons Algernon and Philip had taught me about dealing with journalists didn't seem to make sense in a bizarre situation like this. I didn't even know what they were there for.

"Hold on," shouted a photographer from the windowsill,

"could you do that waking up bit again? I didn't get enough."

I looked at him incredulously. More cameras clicked.

"How does it feel?" asked a woman in a green hat. I shrugged, thinking maybe I was dreaming after all.

"What did the Princess say to you?" asked someone else.

Questions were coming from all sides. One of the reporters was even peering in my wardrobe. Step by step, they took me back through the previous evening at the Spastics Ball, telling me the girl I had grabbed to dance the Rave with me was the Princess. News to me.

I answered their questions then as best I could, only half-awake. It seemed ironical that I had forgotten all I had been taught and there, in bed, bubbled over with the untutored Dan Gabriel, Thickley knew and loved.

The photographers wanted shots of me with my guitar and I had to do the Rave for them as well. I settled down to breakfast after some of them had gone, ignoring the others. My aunt brought me the plate, the cameras popped, and I poised my knife and fork ready to attack the bacon and egg. No chance. A photographer whisked the plate away and got my aunt to bring it back so they could take another shot. I was choked.

After breakfast, they put an apron on me, shoved a plate in my hand, gave me a drying-up cloth, and got their cameras going again. They said that this was a natural story, but it needed photographic colour. A picture of me drying dishes in an ordinary council house, just like an ordinary teenager, the morning after I had taught the Princess to dance the Rave, was a great gimmick. The fact that I never did the drying up when I was there didn't seem to bother them.

If I really said all the things attributed to me in the papers the next day, then I'm surprised. I reckon those journalists, having seen me and heard me mutter one or two normal pleasantries, quickly decided on the image they were going to present. They picked out my most outstanding characteristic—in this case my naivety—and wove their own idea of me around that.

This must be the way personalities get projected. Whatever Algernon and Philip had made me do, they couldn't make me fool journalists. I couldn't have acted naively for instance without sounding utterly phoney. As it was, I was genuinely in the dark about all this fuss. So the legend sprang up about my artlessness.

Time and time again, as I climbed higher up the pop ladder, it was obvious from some of the press reports that journalists had just rehashed something they had read about me from older press cuttings, adding their own views in keeping with my image. That first encounter with the press created an image, a tag, and the Danny Gabriel I've had to live with, even now. Even Mary here believes it, and she knows. I suppose I shall never really lose the monster.

My management were delighted, of course, and the big time project got under way.

"You'll have to watch those photos," said Algernon. "Always try to look your best when the press are around. If possible, make sure that photographers are genuine pressmen; get John to see their press cards. You might find some flyboy coming backstage for your picture and within a few days it will be on sale outside the theatres and you won't get a cut.

"It would be an idea to sew up the photographic business before you start. So many stars lose a mint of loot because they don't think about this. Every theatre you play when you're on tour, you'll find that there are men outside selling photographs of you at 2/6 a time. That's nearly 2/6 profit to them you know. If you make sure that only authorised pictures of you are on sale, and charge a royalty for that authorisation, you'll do okay. After all, if it weren't for you, those people wouldn't be making any dosh at all, so you're entitled to take a commission.

"With this press campaign under way under its own steam," said Algernon, "it'll be my job to keep your name in front of the public all the time. There is a natural curiosity about you now, which will help. A subtle way I could do it is to announce to the press that I'm your publicist and then have you deny it—you'll get a big plug that way.

"But one has to be careful—more singers have been ruined through dodgy publicity than I've had hot dinners. When you are on top, it's very easy to have a lousy publicist and not know it. All he does is take credit for stunts the press boys think up themselves. It's the groundwork that counts."

Algernon was the fourth man to join the Danny Gabriel Organisation dedicated to exploit me for every penny I was worth, and more. The organisation, the entourage, the publicity, every engulfing facet of popdom, tended to obscure from the general public, and from me at times, my own very genuine love of music.

Throughout my career, I took the deepest possible interest in the musical side of everything I did. I listened to every tape, every disc, every song, every note, with an avowed intention to improve each time. I went through agonies selecting the right material for record tracks. I didn't get that privilege immediately, but had to fight for it. My record company were inclined to regard me as a money making robot there to sing whatever they suggested.

The record-contract I signed within a few days of hitting the headlines (it didn't occur to me then that it wasn't my talent they wanted, just my topicality), was a standard one. To me it was, you know, the first time a man tasted milk straight from a cow, something fantastic like that.

It was a contract for one year, renewable yearly for five years. The option to renew or break the contract was completely on the side of the company. So, if my first record was a success, I'd be tied up for five years, or part, depending on the whims of the company. I had no official say in my recording career once the contract was signed. Royalties (one penny per disc) were to be paid quarterly. The records would be released all over the world—America, Europe, Australia and the Far East.

I suddenly found that I'd got an agent then. Bernard, sticking out for the best man, did a deal with the Debroy Martin Organisation, one of the two biggest show business agencies in the country. My representative there was to be Art Cohen. It was Art's job, Bernard explained when I enquired who was this additional man on the payroll, to negotiate all contracts on our behalf. All my TV, radio, film and stage bookings would be through Debroy Martin. Because they were a respected agency with considerable power, I would be earning far more money through them than with other people. They were to take ten per cent.

Records being the main promotion peg for a singer, Debroy Martin must have been swayed in signing me by the quick way Hipdisc got me recording. I went to the session at Emecca Studios in Chiswick full of apprehension. The actual studio I was recording in, and where I made all my later discs, was the size of a huge barn. The walls and ceiling were padded to help with the acoustics, and two huge curtains drawn across the studio, split it into three sections.

It was that large to accommodate the fifty piece orchestras which sometimes recorded there. Microphones had been set up for us at the top end of the studio, where we could be observed from the glass-panelled control room high up the wall overlooking the entire studio. A number of people, journalists, my management team and friends had come along to watch the disc being cut. They sat down along one side and were warned by the recording engineer not to make a sound when the red light was on.

This recording engineer tested our mikes while we played a few notes. There were four of us in the group now; a drummer, a bass and a rhythm guitarist as well as myself. Between us, we could also play the organ, piano and harmonica. A man with rimless spectacles and thinning hair came down from the control room. He was my A & R (artist and repertoire) man, and it was his job to produce my record. He worked full time as the record chief of Hipdisc, and his word was law. Over the years, since giving up his own career as a bandleader, he had gained a reputation as a hit maker. His assistant was a young man I recognized from the pop papers—Brett O'Shea, himself a top guitarist.

After we had run through our number, "Rocking Rave", a couple of times, Harvey Price, the A & R man, told us to tape the backing first. Because we all sang in this number it was technically impossible to record it on one tape and get perfect reproduction. We recorded the backing first and then with the backing played to us over earphones, we dubbed the vocals. This seemed a roundabout way of doing things, but was one I had to get used to. The instruments were recorded on different tapes and the finished record was created when all the tapes were merged together at a midnight session after we left.

The number of times one attempts a recording is called a "take". With experience, I discovered that it takes eight or nine attempts to get a record really perfect, although on one occasion I needed over twenty takes to cut a difficult number. Several things can spoil a take, and they are not all the singer's fault. Someone might cough in the studio, the sound balance might be wrong, or the tape machine might need adjustment. It took us six takes to record the backing for this disc. After each complete take we heard the result over the playback system and listened to Harvey's points on how he thought we could play it better.

When he was satisfied, he put me into a sound proof box, and the boys in another. These boxes are like hardboard cells, slightly larger than broom cupboards. The microphone snaked down from the ceiling, about three inches away from my mouth. I was given some earphones and heard the music being played. I picked out the bars for my cue.

Luckily, this was a number I knew back to front, so I could tackle this bitty technique of recording fairly well. It seemed a shame that for perfect reproduction, it was necessary to dispense with spontaneous recording on which we got more feeling. Although one can achieve technical brilliance in a recording studio, for my money I preferred the carefree rip-it-up, raving atmosphere we generated on stage.

Sweat broke out on my palms as I perched on the stool and waited for the red light and Harvey's cue. High up in the control room, I saw Harvey sip at what looked like a glass of whisky. I made a mental note to get John to bring some along for me next time I visited the recording studio. The red light was on and I could hear my guitar pounding out the infectious rave rhythm. I sang softly into the microphone.

I took four takes to complete my bit. After the initial shock of not believing that I sounded like I do on disc (during which time I suddenly wanted to be pitching hay into the trailer on Thickley Farm) I got used to this strange sound. It wasn't bad, not bad at all. The boys recorded their bit, dubbing the vocal backing. The final take knocked me out. Although it was so contrived and calculated, it really swung. They said that the balance wasn't perfect yet, but as far as I was concerned it sounded really professional.

I recorded one more number that evening, using a much better technique. I mentioned to Brett O'Shea that I preferred to be more spontaneous. He offered to take over lead guitar so I could sing at the same time as the music was being taped. So I sat in the sentry box again, this time facing the group to hear them properly, and recorded "Rave With Me". Amazingly, we cut this in three takes and it turned out to be my first and best-ever seller.

For me and the group, a record started when we got a number as it had been written by the composer. We then had a rehearsal during which we learnt the chords, the chord changes and the melody. Although I eventually gave up accompanying myself on disc, I liked to be with the group during every stage of the construction of a number so I could get the feel of it.

Playing a tune to ourselves, we worked out a suitable arrangement. Our arrangement wasn't our copyright. The composer still collected all the writing royalties whenever his number was played, even though it might have been our arrangement which made it a success.

With each recording, including the titles on my LP, we tried to think of new ideas, new sounds, different rhythms which we could incorporate. We liked to give each of our numbers a completely different structure, and yet still retain the basic "earthy" rave sound, which made me famous.

Everything was worked out between my group and myself, and we never actually wrote anything down. Putting the arrangement down on paper would only have been useful if someone else was going to use it, but since we were all working together, it wasn't necessary.

Sometimes session men would be brought into play on my discs, or a professional vocal group. Session men are the backbone of the recording business. They are all experts in most musical fields—jazz, strict tempo dance music, instant twang or symphonic work. There are about two hundred of them in the business, each man dependent on being thought of when a particular sound is required.

They lead a fairly hazardous life, but one they wouldn't swap for steady band work. They get called in by someone known as a "fixer" who is asked by the record producer to lay on the extra musicians required. For a session, a musician earns about seven pounds ten shillings a time. If he is busy with TV jingles, records (often with overtime!) film-backings and part-time band work, he can earn around a hundred pound per week.

As I got more knowledgeable about recording, I was able to make my own contributions in the way of opinions and suggestions. Brett O'Shea—who worked for the company on a freelance basis—had come in on my disc to assist in the production of this essentially new sound: the Rave. Although Harvey Price was a great A & R man, he was naturally not so well attuned to the teenage taste as was Brett, who was only twenty himself.

Brett had made a number of hit records as a solo instrumentalist but felt the need to develop in the technical side rather than the fame field. Brett became my regular recording manager and was responsible for all my records, failures included. At that first session, I would never have believed that within a few months I'd be up in that control room listening to playbacks, saying such things as "Could we change the chorus phrasing here? Let the boys do it alone, slower and slurring more to get the country effect."

Many singers prefer to record in the evenings, often working until after midnight. They claim that their vocal chords are more relaxed then and that they can work better. I think that is just nonsense.

I know that working on stage every evening meant that

my voice was probably more flexible in the evenings, but for myself, I always felt much more eager for work and better disciplined in the morning when I had just got out of bed. As far as I was concerned, I was prepared to sing, perform, play, whenever it was asked of me. We eventually found that the afternoons suited me best, providing I could be delivered to the studios reasonably sober.

The first session, like my press conference, impressed most people. One paper commented that it was "pleasant to watch an artist like Danny Gabriel in action. No tantrums, no temperament, no timewasting. Just solid hard work allied to a lot of talent."

Brett O'Shea took me off with him that night. I'm glad he did, because I was fed up with the hangers-on I was gathering around me before I'd even got a hit record. We drove up to Soho. It was late by that time, and the pubs were beginning to close. Although I wasn't craving for it, I was feeling very thirsty. Brett solved the problem by flicking open the glove box and producing a bottle of brandy. He must have been impressed by the way I knocked it back.

"You know," he said, as we were crawling through the Piccadilly traffic, "I reckon there's more to you than meets the eye." He raised his own eyebrow enquiringly. "You and me could probably have a ball."

It was five o'clock the next morning when we eventually got to Brett's flat at Finchley. What we had done in those hours since leaving the studio set the pattern for most evenings I had off. Brett, as well as being a brilliant musician, was a moody complex character. He found his relief in people. He loved meeting new people, drawing them out, adopting some of their characteristics for himself, and then moving on.

He had the happy knack of adapting his personality so that in a way it reflected a stranger's own. If he was with a poet, then the poet would see Brett as a kindred spirit. If he was with a tramp, Brett would be a tramp; if he was with a duke, Brett would be as aristocratic as he could. He liked to see what people wanted and tried to give it to them. I suppose he saw through my guileless facade and decided I needed toughening up. This consisted of piling in and out of various drink and strip clubs until we arrived at his place with two birds we would hate in the morning.

The morning happened earlier than I expected with Brett bursting into my bedroom, a silk dressing-gown wrapped round his wiry body, followed by a Hipdisc messenger and the milkman. He put a record on, chatting excitedly. It was my disc!

"You've got to hear this, man. It's the greatest. I tell you this will make it right to the top."

The milkman and the boy listened while my husky voice pleaded with everyone to rave with me. They were fascinated; I could see their feet jigging about - they had almost started raving themselves! It wasn't long before Brett had pulled in the window cleaner from next door to see what he thought of it, and had dragged me out of bed to teach them how to do the dance. The two birds took a dim view of being woken up so early.

Hipdisc rush-released the disc to make the most of the unexpected publicity, which still lingered from the Spastics Ball. Now I had the lousy task, which every new singer is familiar with, of promoting the disc.

Bernard and Algernon whisked me round all the record paper offices to give exclusive interviews to each one. It was also arranged for me to meet disc jockeys to see if they would plug the disc. One of these was a housewives' choice called Mace Skinner. I went to him at his flat in Baker Street. He seemed a pleasant bloke, friendly.

"Yes, I like your record," he told me, reeking of aftershave lotion, "that's why I wanted to meet you. I like to know what singers are like. That's the point of my programmes, you see. Why people listen to me.

"Disc jockeys aren't thought of all that highly in show business. That's why I try to get entertainment-plus in my programmes. One can't do that by just sticking records on. I like to give little personal anecdotes about singers; say that when he was round at my flat, Danny Gabriel had a bath.

That sort of thing. It's off the beat and the listeners like it. You wouldn't care for a bath, I suppose?"

I stared at him.

"We've got a lot of power in this business. We're kind of brainwashers really. If we play a record often enough, *it's* bound to sell more. And if we don't play it, you've had it. I say, do you like swimming?"

I nodded cautiously.

"Yes, I thought you might. Look, I've got a good idea. I've got a pair of swimming trunks here somewhere. They're too small for me. I could give them to you. That would make a nice personal touch." He rummaged through a drawer, and then held up a pair of canary yellow swimming briefs.

"I think these are the ones. I'll just try them on to make sure."

Before I knew what was happening, this unseen idol of millions of radio listeners had whipped off his trousers and pants and was struggling into the swimming trunks, bollocks hanging out everywhere. I picked up a handy copy of *Melody Times* and studied the charts furiously.

"Yes, they are too small. Would you like to try them on yourself? I mean, there's not much point me giving them away if they're too small for you as well." He was standing in front of me, bollock naked, holding out the yellow trunks.

I stood up, tongue-tied. He pushed me back; I staggered then fell on the settee. Just then - *thank God!* - the telephone rang. It was on the table by my elbow so I reached out and picked it up quickly, just in case he didn't intend to answer. He took it angrily. I fled.

That's an extreme illustration of some of the things I had to go through. Many petty prejudices founded on much less significant grounds resulted in my record not being played on a particular programme, or being plugged to death on another.

Air-time for any artiste, however big he is, is important. The old-pals-act among disc jockeys and record pluggers and other interested parties, plays a small part. Phoney requests to programmes are soon discovered and this, in fact, can lead to a disc being ignored.

Much more important than the BBC set up is Radio Luxembourg. It was essential, Bernard discovered, to wine and dine the DJs, although basically the programmes depend on listening figures so Luxembourg has to give its listeners what they want, and not what the DJ's want them to want.

Within a few weeks of the success of my first disc, I had a Luxembourg programme of my own. This was sponsored by a photographic firm although I personally had no interest in photography at all. It was great fun, very relaxed. We used to turn up for a day's session at the Luxembourg studios in Hertford Street and record as many tunes as we could in no particular order. Afterwards, the engineers cut these into suitable programmes, for which I recorded the links. That sort of calm, unhurried attitude I loved. We did thirteen programmes in three days that way and they drew fantastic listening figures.

When my record came out, it wouldn't have worried me if it didn't make the charts. For a kid like me actually to be on disc, to be able to walk into a cafe and see my record on a juke box, was enough. Already through my short time in show business, I had learnt to revert to my old country manner of accepting things as they happened and with no more attention than they merited. I refused to get excited about the record's prospects—or even mine as a singer.

Bernard investigated the possibilities of giving the record a boost to help it into the charts. To get it somewhere in the top thirty, he said, was important because juke box operators would play it then, and each play on a juke box is yet another plug. He discovered it was difficult to fix the charts through sales, as a disc had to sell 4,000 a day to get in officially. But it wasn't necessary.

Writing about my sound—the Rave—a columnist said: "Everybody in the business, myself included, said it couldn't happen here. But it has—the Rave is the rage of the country . . . Musically this is a return to the pure fountainhead of rock 'n' roll—all the thumping bumping, razzle dazzle gear.

"Back it all comes, cascading like a mountain torrent,

washing away all that sugary fiddle-faddle that has been sapping the vitality of teenage music for the last year or so."

Reading that again makes it all seem worthwhile.

CHAPTER 11

The snag about having a hit record is that you've got to find a follow-up. If that's successful, then the second follow-up can be a re-hash of the first. The momentum should be enough to push it into the top twenty. It's the record after that—when the kids are looking for something new -which makes or breaks a singer.

A singer, I soon learned, has a choice of either keeping the same sound or trying something new. If he tries something new too soon in his career, he might just as well be starting again. That's why, for my third record, I kept pretty much to the same formula. It was a reasonable success, reaching number seven in the charts, but not the number one spot of my first two. Then I had the worry of my fourth record. If I could get a hit with that, then I was assured of a reasonably faithful following.

As it happened, my fourth record didn't come off. It was an American number called "Like Love" and was a complete contrast to the Rave rampage I had been on. Natural interest in me got it into the charts, but I wasn't proud of it as a disc. My next one let me down completely. It was one of Bernard's numbers, "A Place For Romance", an up-tempo teenage ballad. It just died.

Now I'm jumped ahead in time here to the middle of 1963. After the failure of that romantic kick, I put my foot down and recorded one of my own compositions. That was "Let Me Go" which shot straight in at number thirteen and rose to number four. Recordwise I was on the scene again, until a Christmas number came along to bring me down.

Success is a razor-edge in any profession; far more so, I should imagine, in the pop world where being a success is a full-time job and it takes up every minute of the day. A successful businessman, for instance, although he has to keep up the pace at his office and in front of employers, can relax once he is at home with his wife and family. A pop singer who wants to stay in the big time, isn't even allowed to have a wife, and never kids.

I was a very recognizable character in my hey-day, and of course still am, so I had to act all the time. I never did this out of bigheadedness, like walking into a bar and hoping people would recognize me. That wasn't my style at all. In fact I used to slink into places hoping that I wouldn't attract attention and could be my normal self.

It never worked out; someone would always lurch up and start some inane conversation about why his daughter liked me, or why he didn't. This didn't stop just with personal recognition either. I couldn't make a reverse charge telephone call where I had to give my name, without being trapped in a long conversation with the operator.

But I liked the work. When I stopped rushing around I got more nervous than ever, dying to do something. Generally, I had so much on my plate that looking back I don't know how I kept it all up. The only snag about my working so hard, and my drinking which increased daily, was that I used to get very tired. Tiredness brought me down and I used to go on stage wondering how on earth I'd be able to sparkle and give the kids what they wanted.

So I drank more to lift the depression. It was a vicious circle. Being a passive kind of character, there wasn't much I could do about it. And as a star I was inflicted with that kind of parasite known as "yes-men". They were the nearest I got to having friends and for a long time I foolishly mistook them for the real thing.

Many people when they hear a pop singer grumbling, immediately counter-grumble with a comment on the ridiculous money he earns. My income from such sources as record sales, stage, radio, and film performances, composers royalties, royalties on things bearing my name (plectrums, advertising and magazine articles) must have averaged the £1,000 a week Bernard had targeted.

I never talked money but left that entirely to my manager. I trusted him so much that I had an arrangement with him to invest a lot of my own personal earnings. The early effects of having money were negligible. I was right at the top for several months before I even got round to buying new equipment for my group. For one thing, it all happened so fast that I didn't have much chance and in the beginning the money was slow to trickle through because of contractual delays.

Of the one thousand pounds a week, four hundred pounds went straight away in percentages to my agent and manager. That left me with six hundred pounds. Out of this, I had to pay my backing group, which usually cost one hundred and twenty pounds. There was then the cost of petrol for running my car (fantastic, as I averaged several thousand miles a week on tour) and hotel bills. My car—a Rover—set me back a few weeks' pay.

I spent a lot on clothes as well, not out of vanity, but out of necessity to appear smartly dressed on-stage and in the street. Each new tour called for a different stage-suit so that I could avoid getting dull presentation-wise. For personal clothes, I liked gear that was both casual and smart at the same time. I must have bought up the entire stock of a John Stephen's shop during my career.

I had to employ a permanent secretary for business purposes at twelve guineas a week, a part-time publicist at eight guineas per week, a fan club secretary at eight pounds, and my road manager, John, at an official fifteen pounds per week, although I upped this to twenty pounds myself. There was my own personal spending money (most of which went on drink) of twenty-five pounds a week. On top of that there were such things as income tax, telephone bills, the return of Bernard's money spent promoting me in the beginning, solicitor's fees, and the most important man in the financial set-up, the accountant. For seventy-five pounds a year, this man handled everything; including all my bills which went straight to him.

John, who worked it all out one night, reckoned I was showing a clear profit after taking care of everything including tax and those conners I couldn't say no to, of seventy-four pounds per week, out of that thousand pounds. If I hadn't loved the business so much, I reckoned I would have packed it in. The work I was doing and the deterioration of mind and body, were worth more than ten pounds profit a day!

Not all managers worked on the arrangement I had with Bernard. There are some who are appointed by a singer himself to handle his affairs. Their percentage is lower than what I was paying Bernard. The other type of manager actually employs his singer. Today, this is a rare arrangement but when pop music first started, a few shrewd people decided to make a business out of it. Finding likely lads, these managers offered them a five year contract to stardom, starting at a weekly wage, increased yearly, regardless of whether the singer was actually working or not. The first week's wage (for doing about the same amount of work as I was) was often as low as twenty pounds a week. This would rise over the years to, say, five hundred pounds per week.

New pop singers jumped at a chance like this, and I think I would have done, for on the surface it seems to offer some security. In actual fact, of course, it didn't. The first year, a singer could be a big money earner and then fade away completely. Naturally, these shrewd managers made certain that there was an option-clause, on their side only, to break the contract, which they did when the singer dropped in popularity.

A variation on this theme were the managers who signed up groups and took over their personal life as well. The method here was to provide the singers and groups with board and lodging in a huge house rented by the manager for them. The singers were even allocated their own packet of cornflakes and their own bottles of milk. Transport was provided for the groups and they played at dances throughout England, all actually promoted by the manager.

So the manager was raking in the cash from promoting dances, and saving it by featuring his own singers. Reasonably well-known names could have commanded forty-five pounds an appearance if booked by an independent promoter, but under this system, they were forced to work for their own managers/promoters and probably earned him sixty pounds per night. Their actual pay at the end of the week, after deductions had been made for food, board and travel, was often as low as seven pounds per week. I know for a fact that some talented singers are still trapped like that through five-year contracts they signed two years go.

During the early days of pop, some unscrupulous promoters decided to economize on backing groups, whom they thought of as the scum of popdom. Using the glory of being in show business as bait, they picked up musicians of suitable ability in coffee bars and offered them work at, say, twelve guineas a week each. The youngsters, probably apprentices by day and musicians by night, jumped at the chance.

At first, all would seem well. The group had three nights a week to play at local dance halls. Their twelve guineas was easy money. Then came the step when the promoter offered the group a wonderful opportunity—the chance to tour with a stage show. Their job was to back all the artistes on the bill, two shows a night, six nights a week.

When the tour started the group discovered what they'd let themselves in for. Out of their wages they found that they were expected to pay their hotel bills, and contribute towards their transport fares to each show. They also had to stamp their own insurance cards. This meant that for a week's work they received about four pounds. Being famous and signing autographs was no compensation for those sort of wages. If they objected, they were replaced.

Philip Le Tissier, who had moulded my act, landed a contract with an independent television company to produce a pop show throughout the spring of 1962. It was scheduled to go out on Saturday evenings. It was this show which finally put the seal on me being a top star. Philip built the whole show around me. All the other acts were well known names, different ones each week. I appeared every show. As I was just a beginner I was an unknown quantity to the audience. Philip created what he described as "a figment of his imagination" with me.

Throughout the first shows, during which I only did one number each week so as not to saturate the screen, I didn't speak a word. I was the silent mystery boy, a sexually-dynamite seraphic infant. My sex appeal lay in my lack of interest in it. Philip would rehearse me for hours getting just the right disdainful glance from me when I was surrounded by girl dancers, but at the same time bringing out a roguish twinkle in my eyes. He was always focusing the camera tightly on my eyes and, as I had a good complexion, the results were not too bad. During those eight weeks, Philip managed to build up such suspense with my item, that people were positively panting to hear me speak.

Even my mistakes on that programme were planned. Once he made me come in on a number too soon, so that the viewers would feel my enthusiasm and believe in me as being so natural. The fan mail the following week was staggering with people pouring out their devotion. Another time, the camera focused on me too long after I had finished a song. That way, viewers thought that they were seeing the real Danny Gabriel. Sometimes, I'd be seen in the background stalking round the crowded set utterly alone, with no one taking any notice of me.

I enjoyed working in television. I didn't get nervous, only suffered a little from camera tension. My usual cure of a swig of brandy didn't help at all really; but I wasn't going to believe that. It took me ages to get used to make-up, though. The only consolation was the efficient unintentionally sexual touch of the make-up girls.

When people meet me after seeing me on TV, they are surprised that I am so small. Smallness comes out in a strange way on television, especially if you are an idol. Fans just didn't think of me being a human being resembling them. Everything about me had to be larger than life, including my height. *Stuck in this bed so long, I reckon I must have shrunk!*

About the end of May of that year, I was right on top. My record was number one, I was doing the television show, and had started touring. The press loved me, my public loved me, and I was happy. Apart from my natural inclination towards girls and drink which, under strict control by John, at the time didn't present a problem, I fitted in perfectly with the innocuous image the public wanted. Then Jan, my lesbian girlfriend, turned up and announced that she was pregnant. I was the father.

CHAPTER 12

It had to happen. Everyone knows that feeling of life going fantastically well and wondering what the price is. If Jan had breathed a word about this to the press, I would have been well and truly lumbered.

She came backstage at a show I was doing at Walthamstow, to drop the bombshell. I was delighted at first. The implications just didn't click. John was there straight away, asking who else knew, whether she was certain, how long to go and all that jazz. He avoided asking what she proposed to do for it seemed obvious that Jan regarded the whole set-up as my responsibility and wanted something done about it.

Bernard was summoned from Brighton for a conference. If the news got out, he said, I would be finished. Any pop singer, whether he had a "clean" image or not, would be in the same position. I could afford, we decided, to have Jan on the payroll in return for her silence. From her point of view, that would have been a more profitable arrangement than exposing me to the *Sunday Horror*.

John was chosen to dissuade her from speaking to anyone, and to find out how much she would settle for. This was a clumsy way of doing things, almost admitting that she could blackmail me if she wanted to, but it seemed the only solution.

Bernard, who was furious and read the riot act about how sex would ruin me (*personally, I couldn't think of a nicer way to be ruined*) reckoned Jan would eventually have the child adopted. The payments to her would only have to be kept up so long as I was in a position to be harmed by being exposed. He figured that after three years, my image would change slightly and it might even be good for me to have some indiscretion revealed. It would make me seem more human. Bernard must have been so surprised because he hadn't reconciled the real me with the image he had created.

Only John properly understood the corrupt person I was becoming and it distressed him a lot, I realise now. I really should have been a better friend and returned his devotion with the sincere affection he deserved. I took his whole life in the end; he married Jan.

It was something they worked out between them without any prompting from Bernard. I couldn't make out if there was any love involved. Jan accepted John because he offered an unconditional security and John married Jan to save my name and because he was kinky about bringing up my son. They called him Daniel. They are still together and their marriage is growing stronger every day.

I've seen Daniel a couple of times and I feel remarkably detached about him. Sometimes, lying in here, I get to thinking that I want him with me, but mostly he is just another private little baby. John's got a living souvenir of me now; I hope he sees that his Daniel makes a better job out of life than the prototype did.

Jan should have served as a warning to me, but she didn't. There's so many queers connected with show business that I, for one, wasn't going to tone down my sex life. I found I could accept queers (and I had to with them round me all the time) only if I had a full and normal sex life myself. Not that they ever propositioned me directly. I treated it all as a joke—part of the act. I used some of their camp expressions and joined in their jokes.

I don't know why there are so many bent people on the pop scene. Do people go into show business because they are queer, or do they turn queer because of show business? Some of the rocksters I've worked with sleep around a bit, but I'm sure they aren't really queer. They're just normal lusty blokes who, because they are normal, are prepared to tolerate a bit of "kinky trade".

Not me, though; girls are my sole sexual preoccupation. For the outsider, it must seem a simple thing for a teenage idol to get a bird, hump her, and then be on his way. It should be a case of sex every morning, noon, and night. But not all girls fancy that, for a start.

I've arrived in a town which has a fantastic reputation for easy lays. "Right," I tell those hangers-on who are always present, gloating at being close to a star, "Get me some birds—real ravers. Let's have a scene."

And what happens? They chase around the town for nowt. Some girls, when asked if they want to sleep with Danny Gabriel, just don't know what to do. I remember actually going to bed after a show and being telephoned by a hanger-on from a bird's flat to say that he'd got this girl all lined up, and would I come over.

I went, the girl was in bed, waiting. Her mate made coffee and we got chatting. But it was no use. The girl changed her mind or something—didn't want to now.

Other times it was my fault. I've had birds lined up for me at a hotel and bundled them straight off to my bedroom. They've been a bit surprised like, but I could have humped them. Then I'd lose interest. It's so easy to feel contempt for a girl who's that easy to lay. And yet still I looked for them.

The snag was that I thought of myself as an ordinary person and not as a "star." I wanted a girl to go with me because I was an ordinary person; but it's hard to impose conditions, and at first I had to take the best of whoever was around. I chased after them—that relentless search for charver—because of an insatiable craving, like my drinking.

Oh, I don't know! I could get them just like that without any preliminaries and I enjoyed it, but it worried me. And then I couldn't get them and it worried me. After a time, because of Bernard's insistence that I didn't jeopardize myself completely by whoring it up all over the scene, I became more discreet, going mostly with girls connected in some way with the business. I found them more tolerable and human, too.

Just occasionally, pop singers come across the easy lay they can feel happy with. She's beautiful, discreet, and knows her art. I met one who was a hotel receptionist. She was eighteen, and had decided quite simply that she wanted me as a man, not as an idol. She conned her way into my dressing room and then let me do the rest. She had tumbled the fact that a *woman* is a woman even to a pop singer, and if the atmosphere is right, they can both enjoy it.

I took her to a party after the show (John had to ditch the girl he'd lined up for me) and we talked. Afterwards, we went back to a flat she had arranged to borrow, and I stayed with her for a couple of hours.

From other musicians who've played the same town, I've discovered that she latches on to all the visiting stars, but only stars. That's all right; I mean, some girls are kinky for cripples, or rugby players. It might even pay some ponce to round up the girls like her and start a call-girl service in all the big towns for visiting pop singers. That way we might feel safe, as well as satisfied.

One of the first girls I charvered when I started touring was the same girl whose house I had woken up in four years earlier in Chester. It was a kind of sweet revenge for me –being able to have the upper hand this time and thus console myself in a weird way for having been so callow.

She came to my dressing room when I was appearing in Chester. I didn't really remember her but the incident itself was firmly engrained on my mind. I had had my usual "tonic" and it wasn't long before I was putting through my plans to get her into bed.

She didn't need much persuading to get her back to my hotel room. John was on hand, as usual, to sort out the night porter. She was a good ride, I remember, and I found the bristles where she had shaved off her pubes, very stimulating.

Touring was an endless round of travelling, eating, performing and sleeping. Before I bought my car, I used to travel with the other artistes in the band coach. We usually picked this up just by the London Planetarium near Baker Street Station. Our instruments were stowed in the boot, or packed in the back of the coach where seats had been taken out to make more room. It was during these journeys that we got to know one another and, as the tour might be playing different towns for six weeks or more, we had to be a fairly affable crowd.

When I wasn't sulking in the back of the coach over something, I enjoyed these coach trips. The waking up in a strange town, having a hurried breakfast and then piling into the coach to race across the countryside to another strange town, fascinated me.

We passed the time by discussing all kinds of things—the players in these pop packages are surprisingly intelligent. I soon realized that a lot of musicians are frustrated idealists, each one with his own plan for solving the world's problems. I let the political and intellectual chat pass me by, preferring to strum my guitar, singing to myself with sheer exuberance at being alive on tour, or to gaze out of the window at the beautiful countryside, my natural home.

Sometimes a poker school started up and the boys gambled ferociously, John included. I tried it a few times but I hadn't hardened sufficiently then to do any realistic bluffing. They could always read from my face the sort of hand I had.

Sometimes we all sang together. The most popular song had this chorus:
Seymour humps our arses, our arses, our arses,
Seymour humps our arses,
And we'll become stars.

After the novelty had worn off, those long journeys in the coach were a drag. I never felt clean—let alone free –spending the whole day cooped up with about twenty others in a stinking bus. And I'm sure I could write a guide to the transport cafes of Great Britain!

In the towns I played at, I stayed at the best hotels. Personally, I found the atmosphere of a boarding house more relaxing but couldn't stay at them because of having to keep up the old prestige routine. There was also a better chance with the girl situation, not to mention the possibilities of after-hours drinking in a hotel.

After shows, I used to sit in the lounge rushing the night porter off his feet fetching drinks for me and the hangers-on. In the end, I used to take my own bottle with me and just sit until I'd polished it off. Then I'd stumble up to bed relying on the ever-present John to get me there without any mishaps.

When there was a crowd of people travelling with me, and I was in the town for a week, I took a suite. For longer seasons I rented a flat. These were the only places I had which I could remotely call home for nearly three years. Travelling around all the time helped to disturb me even more. Away from my village, I felt as though I had no roots or security at all.

To ease the strain of travelling, I eventually persuaded Bernard to let me buy a car. I bought a Ford at first and used to nip around from town to town in that. I hated driving alone and always looked for people to come with me. I was a careful driver, getting more satisfaction out of dawdling than belting along flat out. But I always seemed to be late. So I was often obliged to tear up the road without any more freedom than being in the coach.

Bernard introduced a system of fines to keep me and the group disciplined. Unless there was good reason, whenever I was at the theatre later than thirty minutes before the curtain went up, he fined me five pounds. He also fined my group for such things as no stage shoes, or a forgotten bow-tie or even socks.

That first car did force me to cut down on my drinking, but the good effects were soon lost when I smashed it up. I was driving two girls and John to a party when I thought I saw a car coming towards me on my side of the road. I braked, the road was wet, the car skidded, hit the kerb, overturned, then careered along upside down until it mashed against a brick wall.

It happened very quickly and, apart from the jostling and shrieking going on, didn't seem to mean much to me. The two girls came off worse. My one ended up in the road with a broken thigh. I dropped her after that, and decided not to drive again. John took over, chauffeuring the new car I bought, and I went back to the happy-juice in a big way.

Considering the business my road shows brought to the tatty cinemas normally half-empty each night, one would have thought cinema managers would have done all they could to make us feel welcome. More often than not, they seemed to resent us and went out of their way to make things difficult. There are enough aggravations in being a nomadic popster without their additional high-handedness.

Many times we've found the pass door between back-stage and the auditorium locked. Frequently there wasn't a man on the stage door, either, and we had to hammer on the door until someone bothered to open it. When there was a man there, it was usually some well-intentioned idiot bask-ing in his position of sudden authority, forever pestering me for autographs.

The performer, as far as stage staff were concerned, was never right. I always had trouble with lighting. John had a lighting plot, which he used to give to the electricians to work from while I was on stage. But they insisted on sticking in their own variations.

Frequently there wouldn't be enough microphones, or the mike would break down. Once, the compere of one of my shows complained to the electrician that the mike wasn't even on. The man refused to believe him, and it took a sharp word from the manager at the front of the house to convince him. They could tell the stars what to do, but we couldn't tell them.

The hangers-on who used to crowd into the dressing rooms got me down as well. One night in my room there was the coach driver who, because I was the star, always plagued me; the travelling manager from the cinema chain; the pro-moter's travelling representative; my manager; my record producer; my agent; my stage producer; my publicist; my road manager; the show's promoter; my agent's representa-tive and one or two others, all of whom thought they had a right to be there.

I went to the toilet until they thinned out a bit. All right, I needed them to keep me going, but I preferred to jog along blissfully ignorant of anything being plotted for me, and of the plotters.

From the moment I arrived at a theatre, an hour before a show, I was trapped until the very end. Usually, I joined some of the others on the bill for an impromptu warm-up session on stage. This was great—sometimes we really swung as we waited for the audience to file in.

My relationship with my group wasn't too strong. I accepted them merely as people in the business who worked for me. We were friends and had raves, but only when circumstances threw us together. They went rather in awe of me and I wasn't too keen on associating with them other than musically.

Some singers claim to be great pals with their backing groups but for me, working and travelling with them so much, I preferred to have different people as my friends. Often the only time I saw my group backstage was the group leader dropped into my room before each show to check that my guitar was in tune.

Backstage could be boring, but not so boring as the hotels. When I was playing a week somewhere, I couldn't move out of the hotel for the fans jamming the streets or ready to pounce when I went for a walk. So I used to stay in the hotel, sleeping, charvering, or drinking...or being thoroughly depressed by the sheer desolate boredom of it all.

At the theatre somehow visitors always managed to filter through the security arrangements and reach me. John saw people first to find out what they wanted. If it was someone who knew me, John found out the details then passed them on. This briefing put me wise if I'd forgotten the girl's name and the circumstances of our first meeting.

I liked meeting a few people backstage but found that most of my visitors just came out of unhealthy curiosity to stare at me and then boast about me being a friend of theirs. A lot of local journalists tended to be like this. With a photographer and a notebook they used to pester me for ages with inane questions—the answers they could have got from my publicity handouts, as I did—just as an excuse to gape at me. I was usually anxious to get them out so that I could have a drink.

At the end of a show, the problem was how to get out of the theatre. We had to avoid starting a riot to placate the local police, although many times we got very near to one. The police attitude was never consistent from town to town, and didn't always seem very sensible. Sometimes, they laid on a strong-arm mob at the stage door to hold back the kids. This only created bad feeling. At other times, they would go to the opposite extreme and completely ignore the possibility of anything happening and John and the group would have to bash a way through the fans for me to get to the car.

My sole aim was to dodge fans. This may seem unfair but, Christ! I soon had enough of being mauled and battered to pieces at stage doors. Those kids weren't even gentle with it—several times I've had most of my clothes torn off. Once a girl pulled at my tie so much she nearly throttled me, and John had to slap me back into consciousness. I was nearly ruined for life on another occasion when a determined girl in Dudley grabbed my corey and kept on pummelling it as I was hustled through!

I tried various ways of escaping the chanting, shrieking, madcap lot at stage doors. John used to check all the exit doors as soon as we got to a theatre and work out if we could get a car up to any of them. Those kids had no respect for property, so I rarely let my own car be used. Instead we used a car belonging to one of the hangers-on. For the thrill of helping to smuggle me out, these idiots didn't mind snapped aerials, broken wing-mirrors, and scratched paint-work.

Our favourite dodge was to have a car standing by one of the audience exits, on the opposite side of the stage door. As the audience charged out, I used to pull on an old raincoat and cap, and tag on a few yards behind. It usually worked with the minimum amount of fuss. But in my time, I've had to scramble over rooftops, have the fire brigade (to hose away fans) and go out in disguise. The only trouble about a disguise was that sometimes I'd get recognised, and felt ridiculous caught looking like a beatnik or a tramp.

When I was recognised walking along the street, people reacted as though I was a leper. They stared, they even followed me, but only rarely did they come up and say "Excuse me, aren't you Danny Gabriel?" In cafes, if people weren't sure about me, they played one of my records on the juke box, to see how I reacted. I never stirred.

Because of my naturally distinctive appearance, I was seldom able to go anywhere under my own steam without being plagued by people. John tried to be with me most of the time, as he firmly believed I was incapable of fending for myself.

Officially, John's duties as my road manager were to get me to the theatres on time, look after my gear, and generally see that everything connected with Danny Gabriel ran smoothly. One of his big jobs was buying me shirts. I got through four each day. I would start off wearing one, then change that for the first show. It was always saturated with sweat by the end of the act, so I needed another one for the second house. At the end of the evening I put on another clean shirt as it was usually a few hours before I got to bed. During that time the shirt would invariably finish up with beer stains and lipstick, and be quite unsuitable for the following morning. Laundry was a difficult problem when we were on tour, so John just went out and bought four shirts every day, eight on Saturdays.

The first tour I went on, I was second top of the bill. The star was an American boy who had two hits. Although I worked with him for four weeks, I think I only spoke to him three times. He was a strange lad who was closely shadowed by a silver-haired prosperous-looking Yank. The two of them drove around in a white Cadillac and kept rigidly to themselves.

After eight shows, I was promoted to top of the bill, and the American closed the first half. That was because I was going down better than he was. I don't know if he minded, and I never had a chance to ask him about it. Once, when I was idly tapping out a tune on the piano, he came over to me. "Let me have a go on that, sweetheart," was all he said.

Other Americans I worked with were very pleasant as people. Realising that they were in a strange land, they did seem over-eager to please. They all said how much they loved England, all had that soft milk-and-honey dimpled look, all claimed to be sporting types crazy on exercise and

I should see their gymnastic equipment back home! They all slept just as late as the rest of us, though.

On stage, my own act was a combination of solo vocals and harmonies with the group. Most of the numbers I kept my guitar for, and I played this in a jerky manner which became another of my trade marks. Although it was obvious when I was on stage that I was having a ball, moves and notes had been meticulously rehearsed. I had two announcements to make, which John used to prepare for me as if I had gone on stage without knowing what to say, I would have been lost.

Some audiences never gave me a chance, and it wouldn't have mattered if I hadn't sung a note. I could never understand why those screamers clapped their hands to their heads and sheltered their own ears. I preferred an appreciative audience who got excited when I wanted them to, and then cooled down as I did. Those people who knock teenage entertainers and moan about the passing of the music hall, ought to go along and see a pop music show sometime. I, and all those singers like me, keep music hall well and truly alive.

My favourite trick in the theatre when I saw a bird I fancied, was to let the highly polished metal bits of my guitar catch the spotlight and reflect on to her face. It was fascinating to watch kids in the audience. Some of them would be raving in their seats without realising it and others would be having minor orgasms. I'll give a word of advice here to anyone who is going to a rock show. Don't go to the second house, otherwise you might find that some over-emotional teenager who had the seat before was unable to control herself and tinkled all over the seat! It's a fact!

When I came back from the first tour, Bernard swore at me when he saw the state I was in. I was under the impression that I could get by with very little sleep but, with all I was putting my body through, my angelic face was going for a burton. He quickly put me on a course of "angelicness". The sun-ray lamp was produced with strict instructions to spend so many minutes under it each day. John was bribed to make sure I got to bed early, and alone. I was rushed

down to Brighton or some other seaside resort at every possible opportunity to get some fresh air in my lungs; and—of
course - I was given another strong lecture on drinking.

I had got drinking down to a fine art then. During the day
often starting at breakfast, I would drink lagers. I wasn't out
to get drunk, I just wanted something thirst quenching. At
night, once inside a theatre, I'd start on a bottle of either
brandy, whisky or vodka. I craved for that happy and beautiful expansive high feeling.

If my music was suffering because of my drinking, I reasoned, then it was right to cut it out. But it wasn't. In fact,
when I was high I was relaxed and played even better than
when I was sober—or so I thought. It was only because I was
falling down on the image my operators had created for me
that they were worried. I was beginning to feel contempt for
the machine, reckoned I knew the pitch of drunkenness I
was safe at, and when I reached that, I'd try to stop. But if
pressures got worse, I'd go over the top.

CHAPTER 13

The things that happened next, the events crammed into the few months I was at the peak of the pop profession, leave me limp to look back on them. *Thank God it's all over!* As well as the scars on my mind, the plague on my body, I have got something else to show for it all: a gold disc. That's what "Rave With Me" earned when it knocked up sales of a million.

To milk the gold disc of its full publicity value, Algernon had dreamed up a return visit to Thickley. It was to be on the lines of Golden Boy Comes Home, bags of pathos, sentiment and authenticity. It was a natural.

Of course, this coming-home would have full facilities laid on for the press and TV people who would happen to be there. I hadn't seen my parents for several months. Although I loved them and, when I first started in the business, wanted them to come and see how I was getting on, gradually I got terrified of meeting them. I knew how distressed they would be at the way I was living.

Some stars, of course, revel in having their parents and relatives with them all the time. Those singers whose parents try to get in on the act all the time, pushing themselves into every photo, hanging around TV studios, just sicken me. I'm glad my folks didn't like visiting me.

I didn't think I could face Thickley for very long. My heavy drinking would be pretty obvious in the Queen's Arms and the thought of all those villagers clapping me on the back and talking about little escapades from my past, filled me with horror. I had reached the stage where I hated getting letters from my Mum. I could spot them as soon as they turned up in the office. I don't believe Mum ever bought envelopes—she just used old Christmas card envelopes with a label pasted over the address. The letters were always the same—full of inconsequential gossip, the names of old "friends" who wanted to be remembered, and instructions to take care of myself.

So I prepared for this return pilgrimage to Thickley with mixed feelings. What I hadn't bargained for was how much I had changed. I drove into the little village, under the shadows of the church and round the pump to pull up outside the pub, I was filled with a frightening feeling of nostalgia. I forgot the press boys, following in a convoy of cars, leapt out and raced into the Post Office.

There was Mum. She looked up startled by this tornado bursting into the shop. Dear home—it still had that warm musty smell; it went straight to my head making me feel high at the carefree days it recalled. I hugged Mum deliriously, only to be shaken into reality by the exploding flash bulbs from the eager cameramen. I was deeply conscious of having given way to feelings I didn't know still existed. Algernon was ecstatic.

"Great, great. Oh, this is going to be too perfect for words. What a marvellous home, such a genuine background. I can see you scampering about here as a kid. Now, where's your dad, we must have him clasping you to him. You know, I'm-proud-of-my-boy sort of thing."

Poor Dad was forced to go through the pantomime, and I must confess, I wasn't reluctant to play up to the press people. I had grown used to seeing my photo and name in the papers and reacted automatically when any cameramen were around, remembering my old training to project myself. I tried to get Dad along to the pub for a drink to celebrate, but he wouldn't have it. He was shocked that pub visiting had become part of my life. Mum commented on the fact that I had changed. She noticed instantly how my eyes were harder, something that only she could see.

It had been arranged that I should spend the night in Thickley, but as the day progressed I wanted to get away as soon as possible. The country life I liked, but only to look back on. I was used to more sophisticated pleasures now. The toilet in our back yard for instance, got me down—there didn't seem to be any reason for being that primitive. And on the farm, looking around where I had worked, it all seemed so mucky and inefficient. Looking with different eyes, I couldn't fathom how I'd worked on the farm and been so happy with it. My old boss seemed to be a prize idiot, ingratiating himself with the photographers and keeping on about what a good worker I was.

I hadn't realized how much I'd changed from a Cheshire yoblet to the ogre-like popster I was then. Leading such a sheltered life in Thickley, I was ignorant of the struggles most youngsters go through to reach well-balanced maturity as an adult. My own experiences of life outside Thickley were tinged with the artificiality of show business where glamour and glitter can twist realities, bringing an importance to fads alien to normal youngsters.

Thickley rammed this home to me. Under the influence of show business, I had succumbed to the corruption that thrives in an atmosphere of spotlights, greasepaint, and hero-worship. I drank and shagged too much. Even the youthful contempt I had for the flatterers and parasites of my profession hadn't helped stabilize my instincts. That had pushed me out even further in a way. But after the novelty of my first tour had worn off, I did settle down in one respect: I had only steady girl-friends.

It was difficult finding a woman who had a real love for me. I had a quick turnover in women for purely sexual satisfaction, and then slowed down to look around. Keeping to women connected with the business in some way, I eventually linked up with Rita.

I met Rita in April, 1962, but didn't sleep with her until that Christmas. This doesn't mean that I was maturing in the respect of learning a bit of discretion, finesse, and tact. It was just that it hadn't occurred to me that she might be interested. Rita was a show business journalist, the bright reporter of *Melody Times,* that trade weekly snapped up by pop music fanatics every Friday. It was she who interviewed me when I did the round of the pop papers to plug my first disc I hadn't considered her sexually at all. At that stage, girls were for sleeping with and women were unobtainable. Rita was a woman.

She had all the poise and drive of a successful career girl, and impressed me with her brisk efficiency and pointed questions. When I was touring, or at TV studios, she interviewed me a few times, but I didn't tumble to anything serious going on. One day, when she knew I was in town, she asked me if I'd like to have lunch with her. I did, because I thought it was business. But surprisingly she didn't interview me at all, but talked about herself, about the loneliness of show business and dropped cautious hints to the effect that she was Danny Gabriel's number one fin and wanted to help him if he needed it.

Our friendship developed like a game of chess. She was a' clever girl (no longer a woman in my eyes!) and deliberately created situations which forced me to move in the direction she wanted me to. I had no objection and was intrigued by the possibility of an adult relationship with somebody. Rita did a lot to straighten me out and we both made the most of our affair.

Because she was a journalist, and one well known to fans, it was easy to explain her presence at parties and hotels. Bernard, overwrought in case any of my private life became public, was slightly relieved at my latest acquaintance. It broke up eventually... .when Rita discovered a new teenage idol she wanted to add to her collection.

As well as women and girls, there was a third type of female I came to know intimately—fans. It was easy to recognize a fan, even when she made out she wasn't. I could sense a strained level in her voice—a blur of conversation spouted out unexpectedly, or no conversation at all in which case there was an awkward silence as I had to find words to put them at ease myself. (I was typical in so far as it's rare for a star to be either a good listener or have a large range of conversation.) If a girl's eyes were dilated and she seemed to have difficulty in seeing me, she was a fan.

Fans had this image of someone wonderful in their minds, but when they got up close, they found I was just an ordinary person. I once had a girl practically throw a fit on me when she came into the dressing room while I was shaving. It hadn't occurred to her that I had to shave to keep my youthful good looks.

"It's enough to know that I'm in the same country as you; being in the same house or room would drive me nuts."

That's the sort of things people used to write in their letters to me. I liked those letters for what they did to my vanity—although what some fans swore to do could be frightening. One girl said she would kill herself unless she could bear my child. I don't know if she did.

I had a fan club run terribly efficiently by a dowdy teenager who loved organizing things. Thousands of kids paid five shillings for the privilege of getting inside information on my latest activities, as dreamed up by Algernon.

Fans, I discovered, were quite prepared to suffer a singer with an uncooperative manager. They would write and say "I know it wasn't your fault that I got slung out of your dressing room" or something like that, so I soon started using management as an excuse when I couldn't face up to the kids.

There were certain functions I couldn't avoid though, such as stiffly formal luncheons and receptions. After my gold disc, the big directors of Emecca gave a luncheon in my honour. This terrified me—I had to be so polite in my conversation. At first, the official receptions with civic dignitaries and everyone on their best behaviour fascinated me, especially when I thought that these people had all gathered together in my honour. But after a while, these shindigs became a colossal drag, apart from the advantages of all that free booze. Even then, I had to make out I was only drinking coke, but I dosed it with whisky first!

I was winning honours in every field now. The Mothers' Union voted me as the boy they would most like their daughters to take home for tea. They did this a week after the Mothers' Union suggested the sale of contraceptives should be banned—obviously a recruiting drive. I was also voted one of the country's ten best-dressed men for 1962—a very strange acolade which Algernon had something to do with. Hairdressers, too, said they had cut more D.G.'s (Danny Gabriels) than any other style that year.

These honours, on top of my fantastic success as an idol,

had their effect. I became arrogant, cautious about bestowing any favours. Once I was booked for a charity concert in London. I turned up there with John and was confronted by an organizer who hadn't even heard of me, hadn't got my name on his list for a dressing room, and told me to go and find one for myself as he'd got better things to do.

This off-handed treatment offended me, especially as I was doing the show for expenses only. I walked out. There was a row in the press over that which tarnished my image a bit.

I got very cross with anyone when I didn't get the treatment I thought I deserved. I will say this, though, being so instantly recognizable may have restricted my private life, but it did mean I got better service in restaurants.

I began to believe a lot of the crap the publicity said about me. I began to think of myself as someone capable of doing no evil whatsoever. I looked upon my increasingly degenerate way of life as being exonerated by my image. It was said that I looked too good to last long in the world. I felt that I had to live up to that statement somehow, and began to believe in my early death. I think subconsciously I was trying to stimulate this by drinking so much.

Of course my strange behaviour didn't escape notice. Algernon, when the inquiries arose, hit on the idea of saying I was drugged with pills through being ill. He hinted that the illness although not serious was a chest complaint which had to be looked after carefully. The lies told to preserve my image of purity!

This aura was kept fairly well. That was evident from the approach made for me to pose in choir boys robes for Christmas cards being printed for some national charity. I thought the whole thing was a bit sick, but Algernon said it was an excellent idea—me as a Christ-like image in millions of homes. The week those cards were released and in the middle of the subsequent publicity I caught VD, a venereal disease.

I had a severe attack of gonorrhoea and it was necessary for me to keep off alcohol for a couple of days while tests were made. For those two evenings, I was living in a differ-ent world. I was tensed up, completely unable to relax; I wanted to scream, I was so desperate for a drink. I shouted at people, refused to see journalists or fans and had a furi-ous row with John. When he brought me cokes without any whisky, I threw them at him. My act was lousy, and I played for ten minutes instead of twenty.

The kids knew something was wrong, but it was only then that the full horror of the condition I was in was rammed home to John and Bernard.

CHAPTER 14

Over the months, John had studied my drinking pattern fairly carefully. He noticed that I drank until I reached a certain pitch. After that, I wasn't worried. I could go to sleep, go on stage, do a TV show, or anything quite happily and efficiently. He calculated that my quota before I reached that stage was six bottles of beer during the day and three double brandies in the evening. Over that I was uncontrollable. So that's what they made my ration!

I protested wildly, saying that I was going to drink what I liked if I wanted to. It seemed to me that they were making a lot of fuss about nothing: I certainly didn't consider myself in danger of becoming an alcoholic. My main interest was still my guitar, and I reckoned a little drink gave my playing more punch.

For the next six months, it seemed as though I were living a farce. John, who had settled down in a house in Golders Green with Jan and the kid, couldn't watch over me constantly. He was still very fond of me but I was becoming very unpleasant at times and impossible to keep up with.

Bernard hadn't got the time, nor the patience, to watch me—and he seemed to resent that I should need close attention. So it wasn't very hard for me to ignore their rigid rationing. There wasn't a flicker in my eyes as I blatantly lied to them about not having gone over my quota.

Cunning wasn't the word for the way I behaved. I really tried to be nice to people, to talk in a simple, although sometimes slurred, countryman's way; to look as though I had a childlike wisdom about me and a fatalistic innocence. Journalists and fans found me more articulate, helped by the pre-conceived image they had of me; the management team found me more pliable and responsive. I feigned an interest in what they were doing for me, embracing it with all the vibrant energy my stage act was famous for.

My nightmare of deceit was a dream of perfection for them. Without their supervision I was still knocking it back. I did have the sense to control this and not get into any violent outbursts. People in the pubs around Soho got to know the state I was in and, throughout the towns I visited, so did a lot of other people.

There was now a situation where a word of mouth publicity told the truth behind the façade. Such was the strength of my image that people who gossiped didn't really believe, but liked telling, the story. If you want to find out just what goes on in the exclusive world of a big name, it won't take long to come across somebody who knows somebody who knows that big name. The gossip, although garbled, is probably based on fact.

The ludicrous situation meant that everyone thought I was getting better as I became more deceitful and haggard. Of course, constant drinking was affecting my appearance. My hands were developing a permanent shake. The brightness had left my eyes and I was putting on weight.

To combat the signs of drunkenness such as slurring speech, rolling-walk and rambling-tongue, I acted that way when I could only be sober. Being accepted like that gave me a much greater licence.

To combat the changes in my appearance, the angelic course was stepped up again. I was expected to take daily exercise of some sort. A lot of singers like squash, but I didn't fancy that. I played table tennis occasionally and dabbled with fencing. I liked horse riding and whenever possible could be found at the stables nearest where I was appearing. I liked rowing as well and occasionally went on the Serpentine if there were not too many people around.

Swimming, which I was fairly good at, was out of the question, unless I hired the whole baths for myself. When I tried swimming in public everyone got out of the water to watch me. If there was no chance for open air exercise, then Bernard had me doing press-ups. By then I was drinking hard, only letting up for exercise and massage to combat the effects of it!

Bernard thought a spell by the sea at his home town might help, so he got me a six-week pantomime booking in Brighton. He found a great flat for me on the seafront, which I was to share with Del Semper, the comic in the pantomime. I had worked with him before and got on well with him. He was given instructions to keep his eye on me. John came down to be my dresser and general dogsbody at each performance, but drove back, in my car, to Jan each night.

The pantomime was fun and a new experience for me. I wasn't called on to do any acting, but just came on halfway through the show as Simple Simon. I had no ambition to act or be—as most pop singers publicly claim—an all round entertainer. I wasn't desperate to linger in the business if my popularity as a popster faded. I liked the perks and the money, of course, but I didn't bother to kid myself that I had the talent to do anything more than look cute, sing, and play the guitar.

I liked Brighton. It struck me as being a kind of Notting Hill Gate by the sea, with its quaint Lanes, drinking clubs and odd characters. It's had a reputation in recent years as being a kind of teenagers' playground. For myself, I didn't find the girls any different from elsewhere, but I was struck by the with-it-ness of the boys.

I met a few of these accidentally one evening. John had taken me home in the car and I was supposed to be going to bed. I sat in the lounge listening to a Leadbelly LP, swigging some whisky I had kept hidden. I was a bit high, but mostly restless. I told Dell I was going for a walk.

It seems that Brighton makes its own bedtime. Although it was around two in the morning, there were still laughing couples and packs of blokes roaming the streets. I found a modern-looking coffee bar in the Lanes still open. There were about five people in it. I took the risk and went in.

The occupants, four fellows and a girl, looked at me curiously, but said nothing. I ordered a glass of milk and walked over to the juke box—always my refuge in a strange place. The records were mostly traditional jazz including a whole batch by strange named Americans I hadn't heard of and a collection of Negro folk songs. I decided I liked this coffee bar.

The records I put on impressed the kids in the corner for one of them called me over and asked me what I did, said he hadn't seen me around before. Straight away I felt, well, here was something great. I didn't want to spoil it yet, so I just shrugged.

"You're one of us," said the boy with almost-bleached fair hair, who had spoken first. He wore a black pinstriped suit, continental style. "Come and sit down." He introduced me to his friends who were art students. There was a kid with a beard who I spotted straight away as a phoney. He wore a CND badge and fitted the picture I had in my mind of a typical art student. I blocked him out there and then.

There was also a boy about my age with a definite free-love lecherous look about him. He was cuddling the girl, a French au pair. Another boy, Dave, looked like a rugby player. He was still at grammar school but contemptuous of the whole set up. He spoke slowly and I took to him straight away. The boy with the suit used to be at art school but now he was part owner of this particular coffee bar. He said his name was Keith.

I examined them all quickly. For the first time for ages it looked like I'd got a chance of being accepted as equal by a group of normal teenage types. None of them seemed to recognize me, even though a couple of my records were on the juke box. Thank God I hadn't tried to show off and played those. I told them my name was Dan. It didn't register.

They were obviously trying to put me in some recognizable mould. To them I looked like the smart sort of London-type teenager who could have been called a modernist. Not that I liked modern jazz, but I dressed in an ultra-fashionable style thanks to John Stephens. But so did these kids, although personality-wise they were the type who could have been dubbed "beatnik".

In Brighton at the beginning in the early 1960s, teenagery was still somewhat confused. The teddy-boy fashion had died leaving a legacy of an obvious gap between the labouring type teenager and the schoolboy/tech-college type. Beatnikery, the academic-type Ted, had become the vogue for a while bringing the two rival factions together slightly, although morals, appearance and taste stayed different. What they most had in common was that both types were having their own revolution.

Brighton, the spearhead of teenage development in England, was trying to point a new way, and the kids in that coffee bar were a typical example. They were utterly classless. That they were forerunners of a trend is obvious because today there is no way of distinguishing a man by his appearance for his musical or moral tastes. Most teenagers—itself an obsolete word with nasty connotations; teen-adult would be a better expression—are embryo sophisticates with all the suaveness that goes with having money to spend and the knowledge of what one rates as best.

This merging of the two types is happening all the time and will go on doing so for years. In appearance, teen-adults may all be stamped with the "I am young and modern" brand but underneath, each type still has a different approach to living—and sleeping! It was that which made my new friends in the coffee bar curious to know more about me.

My choice of music marked me similar to them—if my mannerism didn't—so we talked about that. None of them were desperate to know where I came from or what I did; they were obviously prepared to accept me on face value. I told them I was staying down in Brighton for a few weeks, just looking around.

"Have you got money, then?" asked the bearded phoney.

"Yes!" I glared at him. He was nonplussed.

"Well, could you buy me a coffee, then?"

"No, *then,*" I said, turning to Dave and asking him whether he came into the coffee-bar every evening.

"Most nights; depends. There's sometimes a dance at the college, or we go and play billiards in the club, or table-tennis in the pub next door, or ten-pin bowling, or go to the theatre, or the cinema, or the greyhound stadium, or watch wrestling, or have a party or . .."

"What he means is," said Keith, "that there is always

something to do if you want to. The trouble is that most people seem to prefer being bored."

"There's a party on Saturday if you'd like to come," said the lecherous one. "It'll be all night."

This was fantastic. Do you know, I had never been asked to a party in my life because I was me, apart from those times in Chester and Liverpool. I'd been to hundreds since, including some real orgies, but none because people liked what they saw of me and didn't know I was famous.

Being a lonely soul, I could never refuse an invitation to a party, especially if it was given by a more intimate acquaintance. I used to go along, mooch around, spending most of my time at the bar mixing myself fantastic concoctions—anything to get me high and happy.

One party, I was trapped in the kitchen with a bird, fixing myself a drink. I had taken the precaution of locking the door so I could make use of some drink I had hidden. I was alternately snogging the bird and sipping my drink for maybe ten minutes while the party raged.

Yet, when I went back into the living room, everyone had gone, except for John, a boy called Paul and two girls. Well, I always got the impression at places like that, that I was the reason for living, and I tried to share myself around. I spent the whole night darting between the two girls, one in bed, one on the floor, trying to keep them both happy while John slept in the other room and Paul had passed out in the broom-cupboard.

When I was high, I was a real slag sexually. I was good in bed and made sure as many people as possible got personal experience. During my time in the business, my body was tossed from bed to bed with fantastic regularity.

I've even humped a girl stretched out on a train seat on the Glasgow-London express while another well-known pop singer watched. He'd already had his turn.

I spent the rest of that week tensed and excited. Praying that the five people in the coffee bar wouldn't tumble who I was. I deliberately avoided the place, staying in the flat after the show was over. On Friday night, I plucked up courage to go back. I left it as late as possible when I reckoned there wouldn't be many people there.

Luckily, the coffee bar was very dimly lit, so no one took much notice as I walked up to the counter. I saw the boy I liked, Dave, sitting there with another fellow. I didn't see anyone else I recognized. I nodded at Dave, ordered a milk, then joined them at their table. Dave introduced his friend, a sharp Jewish bundle of energy called Tod; a professional gambler at eighteen. Tod gave me a quick glance then launched into a tirade about a dead-cert horse for the next day.

"Put a hundred nicker on it, Danny," he said suddenly, "and you'll get a week's loot for free."

It was impossible for me to expect that I wouldn't be recognized, but I had never anticipated acknowledgement of me to be taken so casually. I was almost offended at being accepted so off-handedly, until it occurred to me that these people just didn't care about my fame. I meant nothing to them. My music wasn't their kind and probably everything I represented professionally was against their principles. But they were prepared to accept me as a fellow young man - ignoring the façade, the publicist's image.

That night, about 4 a.m., I walked along the sea front with Dave. He lived a mile further down than me, and I was grateful for his company. He talked about general things, about Brighton in the season, about his hopes to become a commercial artist.

"It's a profession people sneer at because they think you're being lazy. I don't know why art students should be thought of as weirdies. Just because they want to create something out of their mind rather than with machinery and experiments like technical students."

"I don't know many students," I told him. "Those I have come across have been university types who seem to be so out of touch with reality that you wonder how they can exist. I don't mean because they haven't heard of *me*, but they still seem to be living in the cocoon they were born in at school. They sneer at types like myself, yet you don't."

"Why should I ? Or any of us really. I knew you the moment I first saw you. In fact, I've watched your career for some time, just out of curiosity. I wondered what you'd really be like. I didn't envy you at all. It's obvious the sort of hell you must have to go through every hour of the day."

"If you recognized me straight away, why didn't you say something ?"

"Two reasons, I suppose. I didn't want to embarrass either you or myself in having to explain who you were to the others, and mainly because you would have identified yourself if you wanted to. You told us your name, anyway."

"It's funny for me, talking to someone like you," I told him, feeling mellow with his companionship and the contents of the hip flask I had with me. "In this business it's impossible to have any friends. Old friends from the days before I made the big time have just disappeared. I suppose they are too embarrassed to approach me now I'm a star, and I just haven't got the time to nurture and take the lead with a friendship. And show business isn't a good hunting ground for new friends."

The sea, lashing the pebbles in the biting chill of the early morning air, was a wild background to my mood. With that great shivering expanse of ocean to my left, and the towering Regency flats of Brighton's sea front on the right, I felt poised on the edge of eternity. The roar of the sea and the crisp smell of freedom brought back to my mind the day I first saw the seas from that glade in Wales. I remembered how I discovered the world was big.

That night, through the intensity of opening my heart to a complete stranger, I achieved an intimate therapy I hadn't known before. The world seemed a little bit smaller this time. Dave had his doubts and uncertainties as well and, sharing our own very limited experience, I think we learned from each other.

Dave's friendship and the afternoons I spent with him on the downs, and those early morning walks along the beach, did more for me than my daily quota. Although I had had the opportunity for intellectual-type discussion many times with people on tour and with John, these never seemed to work out for me as those people had axes to grind. Dave, I found, was similar to me in having to bluff his way through to a certain extent in a grasping attempt to learn what other people seemed to know before him.

For instance, he had parent trouble. His parents didn't understand why he stayed out so late at night, every night. His own difficulties made me think more of my folks. But it wasn't just chatting in our friendship. He was able to partner me in billiards, table-tennis, those sort of things. He took me to parties as well. Of course, word quickly got round about his friendship with me, and if I found that there were people at those parties who had just come to stare and watch me relax, then I'd grab Dave and go back to my place.

I went to a party on the Saturday after our beachside walk. It was a big house and by the time I arrived after the show, things were really swinging. The die-hard partygoers, all with girls, were very drunk. There were about a dozen people there, all from the same clique. They didn't bother me at all, so I was soon sufficiently secure and high enough to clamber into bed with the French girl, Odile, and her lecherous-looking boy friend for a sandwich. I vaguely remember Odile trying to decide whom she really wanted. She simply measured my penis, compared it with her lecherous lover's, and chose me.

CHAPTER 15

After Brighton, I started a new television series, and was heard frequently on the radio. I was working hard although, over the months, my records generally weren't doing as well as they used to. My LP released in November, 1962, before the pantomime, had shot up the LP charts but dropped out in February. The failure of "Like Love" and "A Place for Romance" may well have been that the public were beginning to get sick of me through my frequent broadcasts. Maybe I had been over exposed.

Bernard made me change my image by changing my style of numbers, and also getting me to perform without the guitar. Both of those decisions I personally thought were wrong, but against such strong pressure from the dozen or so people running the Danny Gabriel Organization, I didn't stand much chance. I felt I should stick to the beat-up rave kick and leave the ballad work to singers of greater stature.

Bernard laughed at the suggestion that the public might be getting too much of me and said that I should do as much work as possible while I had the chance. When I talked it over with Algernon, he agreed that I should play it a bit cool publicity wise. I was beginning to doubt Bernard's integrity.

I was booked for a big Summer season in 1963 at a town in the North of England. The weekend before I went up for rehearsals in July, Bernard had done a curious thing and booked me on a daytrip cruise to France. Even now I don't know why he did that. True, the money was fantastic, but so was the inevitable outcome. It was a measure of my decreasing importance as a pop singer that my manager was prepared to put me on a boat with thousands of fans and no chance of escape.

There were about ten groups on board, eight of them amateurs from the south coast who'd come along for food and kicks. The other group was one we had worked with before, a gimmick instrumental group who had a few medium-placed records.

From the beginning the whole trip was chaotic. It was an hour before anyone could play as it hadn't occurred to the organizer that our amplifiers and guitars were on a different current to that of the boat. A transformer had to be rigged up. I wasn't supposed to perform till we'd reached mid-Channel. I was getting agitated not only because I was against the whole idea, but also because I hated things going wrong at the last moment.

Stuck in a small cabin filled with the sweaty-gear of ten blokes instead of being able to walk on deck is no way to spend five hours in the Channel. However, it was only a few minutes like this that I was without a beer. Of course, it hadn't occurred to anyone—not even me –that the bars would be open all day!

I went out of the cabin and through the restaurant. Outside on the deck and in the gangways, there were hundreds of kids furiously doing the Rave. I pushed through them to lean over the side and try to get some sea air into my lungs. Of course, it had to happen that just then the group stopped playing, and half a dozen people spotted me. I was soon surrounded by kids clamouring for an autograph.

I wanted to scream. When the music started again some of them left. I pushed my way brusquely through the rest without a word. I wasn't going to put up with being mauled, pestered and pummelled as well as tossed by the roll of the boat for the five hours. I found the restaurant bar, didn't care a damn about the curious fans watching me, and ordered a double whisky and coke. I gulped it down, then quickly ordered another.

I was feeling better now, prepared to have one more drink to take back to the dressing-room where I planned to sit strumming the guitar to help me calm down. I raised the glass to my lips, trying to stop my hand from trembling quite so much. A flashlight shattered my thoughts. One of those curious fans—why hadn't I noticed he was a press photographer?—shouted across "Thanks, Danny. Just wanted a picture of you relaxing."

That was it. I couldn't cope with much more now. Here was

I, supposed to be a clean-living non-drinker, photographed with a double whisky and an alcoholic shake. I ordered another double and six bottles of beer. A waiter followed me into the dressing room (one or two of the boys were there, luckily John wasn't—probably looking for me) and I settled down to drink my sorrows away. The trouble is that drink doesn't drown one's worries, it just keeps them afloat.

I was fairly high when John turned up. He had been searching the whole ship for me and had also had a word with the pressmen who'd questioned him about my drinking. He had denied everything and said that I would prefer no publicity for this trip.

It was then that he discovered that the boat was swarming with pressmen as a real teenage riot was anticipated. This was the first time a Twist & Rave party had been to France and the port we were going to had insured itself for twenty-five thousand pounds just in case. This was the sort of publicity I could do without. Another double was called for.

We had to fight our way through to the makeshift stage. But the time I got there my shirt had been ripped and for a moment I thought my guitar had been damaged. That would have been the end. I slurred my way through a few numbers. The kids, packed closely round me as far as I could see, started Raving at first. But then the crush and curiosity at the way I was performing, got too much for them.

All eyes were turned on me, watching me not with teen-age hero worship—these kids were too callous for that—but with bafflement at my behaviour. It was obvious to anyone including the sweetest schoolgirl, that I was pissed. John dragged me off the stage when he saw how bad things were. The kids were in an angry mood because they thought they'd been let down.

John slung my arm over his shoulder and pushed me staggering through the crowds. I was shouting back at them calling them a load of creeps and swearing at them for the state I was in. I blamed it all on to them, turning on John whenever he whispered to me to control myself.

I must admit he was very patient, ignoring the attendant

cameramen, who were really having a ball. He pushed me into the restaurant, where we escaped the fans. I went up to the bar but John came over and pulled me away.

"Come on, let's go into the dressing room, Danny."

"Don't you bloody push me around, mate," I yelled at him. "If I want a drink, I'll bloody well have one."

He could see that we'd only have a scene in front of the nation's gossipers. I held the best hand.

"Sure, sure—but let's have it in the dressing room, shall we ?"

"Why in the dressing room? The bar's here, isn't it ?"

"Okay, have it here if you like. I'll buy you a single."

"A double."

"Nope, a single. You can have a double in the dressing room."

"Afterward the single?" (*I was cunning!*).

"No—instead of the single now. Come on, don't let's mess around."

I was tiring, I just wanted to collapse. John knew me better than I did myself.

He put his arm round me gently, cooing: "Christ, this is a bloody awful do, Danny. I don't know how they expect you to put up with everything. You've done well considering the poxy state we've got ourselves into. Only a superman could have played like you did just now with all those kids there. And you're human, Danny. You're not really a superman. Come in the dressing room, and relax. Without these people aren't around you can unwind."

He lead me off calmly; the cameras still clicking.

"I could use a couple of doubles, John," I said imploringly. "Please help me John."

I rocked backwards and forwards with the pitch of the boat. It was a few seconds before my eyes focused on anything. Then I saw it was the sea, coming up and down, up and down, splashing against the porthole. I felt sick.

It was me vomiting all over my guitar case which gave John the idea of issuing a statement. Somehow he had to play down this story, keep the fact that I was drunk from the general public, and get me out of this mess as quickly as he could.

As far as I was concerned, I had no qualms about breaking contract or anything like that. I spewed for a while, and then gulped down the brandies John provided. I guess he decided that it was no use fighting me now. He was stern enough but every time I launched into a plea for a drink, even if it took half an hour, I got the drink eventually.

A private ambulance (laid on by John over the ship's telephone) met me when the boat reached port. To be in keeping with the brief statement John issued to the press saying that I was suffering the effects from drugs prescribed for me for my chest complaint which had been aggravated by the sea trip and overwork, I was carried to the ambulance by stretcher.

John pleaded with me to be quiet and not start singing and shouting while they carried me off. I obeyed him, although an astute French photographer got a marvellous picture, which was splashed over the continental papers of me winking at his camera.

I was driven to a nearby airport sleeping drunkenly now, and flown back to England in a chartered plane. Bernard was at Ferryfield Airport, Lydd, with a hired ambulance to meet me. I had recovered enough to stumble to the car supported by Bernard and John and shielded from the press by some other side-kicks I hardly knew.

The big problem was not to overplay the illness side of things, and yet still retain a bit of authenticity. It was decided to issue a very truthful statement from my doctor saying I should rest for a few days to recover but would be quite all right afterwards.

Amazingly it may seem, but that publicity didn't turn out too badly. The crowds who flocked to my summer-season, all seemed to love me. Maybe they came like vultures hovering, waiting for me to collapse in front of them but nevertheless they came.

I was sharing top billing with Lucy Locket, one of the new girl singers whose own record was the then big number. As soon as I met her I knew she was me. Apparently I'd been an idol of hers for ages and, now that she had got into the business and learnt a few home truths about singers, including myself, she was raring to go.

She was a beautiful girl with glistening black hair and, this I found exciting, a kink for black leather. She had a complete outfit in black leather, from boots, a skirt, a wrap over, a coat and gloves. My God! She was a knock-out !

As you can guess, it wasn't long before we were playing that fabulous game of picking each other up. With an obviously longer term friendship (we had the whole summer season), I loved the coy moves involved in getting a girl into bed. It was great for me to find an attractive girl who would play hard to get, especially when I knew I wouldn't fail to get her in the end.

Our affair lasted the complete summer season and ticked on between one night stands afterwards. The ironical thing was that she had a different publicist to me who also handled an up and coming singer called Tavy Tender, and he put out that Tavy and Lucy were a mutual admiration society, while I was actually living with her! I gave that girl my entire self and was rewarded with an intensely happy, almost non-alcoholic, few weeks. I even wrote her poems.

Swayed in the dark in your dreams before you
At the foot of your bed, I slithered
Out of my jeans and stepped down on to you
As a body alert, as your body quivered
And beckoned, arms open and upright, desperate.
Swiftly, silently, there: hot contact,
Leather slashed flesh, nudging like a blind lizard;
Lingering in your gasping mouth.
Tongue round the top, tasting, tickling
Three enormous yawns which shivered
To the root of the deepest pit in hell;
A promise, a promise, a bellow,
And a draught of life trickling.
Like the morning tears to the heart

As I creep exhausted away, withered
Out of the dark, and your dreams before you.

Lucy worked wonders for me. The new pleasure I had found in living bubbled over into my work. Bernard, very cautious now about the property he was handling became overbearing in my eyes. He insisted on my doing certain numbers I hated in my stage act, because he thought they went down well.

I knew they didn't and took them out when he wasn't in the theatre. He came up unexpectedly one night, and we had a furious row about me trying to do things by myself. I wanted to cut one of my own numbers as the top side of my next disc, and he didn't like the idea of that.

I took matters into my own hands and talked it over with Brett O'Shea, my record man. Brett agreed with me. I recorded my number "Let Me Go" which stuck me firmly back in the top bracket of the charts. Bernard was cooling towards me. In a way, it would have been the theme song for our relationship then.

Let me go, let me go
Let me leave, let me rave, you're so
      Demanding with your love, but my teenage love
      Your love is not enough
      To keep me, so
Let me go, let me rave, let me go."

Okay, the lyrics are trite but the tune was fantastic. The success of that disc didn't go unnoticed in the film world. Bernard had occasionally been approached by film producers to see if I would take part in one of those pop music epics they kept on churning out. It was Bernard's view that I didn't need that sort of exposure and that, if I did go into films, it would have to be for a very high fee.

He wasn't exactly confident about my acting abilities and reasoned that if something did go wrong, we should have been paid enough to make even a flop worthwhile. After my initial success in the charts the film offers stopped, and Bernard wasn't keen on chasing after chances himself. So it was a surprise to me when he mentioned that I'd been offered a role in a new big budget musical picture called "Happy Heidi".

I was at Bernard's flat when he told me. We were talking about my drinking as usual, and I was getting really bugged. Then casually he mentioned this offer and said that he was going to turn it down as I obviously wasn't capable of handling one of the star roles in a musical extravaganza.

I was thinking the same thing myself but I didn't like him saying it. I was fed up with Bernard ruling my life. *What did he mean?—I wasn't capable!* I phoned up Lucy to ask her views. It turned out that she'd been offered a part as well. That settled it.

Filming was to begin in October and would finish at Christmas. The framework of the plot were the activities of a girl called Heidi who started a worldwide charitable organization run by young people. There were all sorts of tensions connected with it as an excuse to feature some of the world's leading stars, as well as the top singers.

Seymour Royce had contributed some of the songs. It was fantastic company for me, and Lucy, to be appearing with. If I didn't come up to standard, it would be embarrassingly obvious. When I saw the script and really thought about having to portray someone on screen, about having to act and not just be myself, I wanted to abandon the whole thing. But I was determined to go through with this, just to spite Bernard.

Before I began filming, I had to have a medical check-up. The doctor confirmed that I was physically a pretty fair specimen—the debauchery of show business hadn't destroyed my sturdy little body completely. Mentally, the doctor didn't have a clue; that wasn't his business anyway. But he did discover that my heart was weak through all the drinking I had been doing and that my gonorrhoea was still lingering!

That Friday, Rita's gossip column in the Melody Times

said: "I hear my favourite clean living ex farm boy popster, Danny Gabriel, has been passed A1 for his part as a clean-living farm-boy in the new mammoth musical "Happy Heidi". Even though he hasn't acted before, Danny should feel at home with all those cows".

Filming isn't glamorous. I found it sheer hard work. I soon realized that Bernard was right: I shouldn't have taken it on. I don't know what my acting was like; no one has said anything yet. It was the boredom that got me. I had to be at Pinewood Studios at seven o'clock each morning.

After the make-up business was all over, there was my script to study, until I was wanted for rehearsing or filming. Often that wasn't until the afternoon if the schedule went haywire, but I had to stick round just in case. Cooped-up in my dressing room, it's no wonder I began to go a bit berserk. I pushed the drinking over my regular quota now, unless Lucy was with me. But she was tiring of the demand I made on her spare time; and sex, although fabulous, wasn't enough to keep us together.

Whenever I could, I walked around the studios. I found it pleasant being with so many well known faces, almost as though I were an ordinary face in the crowd again. No one, except studio-staff occasionally, pestered me for autographs or pointed as I walked by. I didn't feel a leper because of the attention I attracted and everyone seemed remarkably friendly.

The film production team seemed to consist of frustrated idealists each with an ambition to join a kibbutz in Israel. I would have loved someone to have walked around with me, though, or to talk to in the dressing room. John came down sometimes and visited his old friends, since that was where he was working when he met me two years before, but as there wasn't the work for him and he didn't tumble the extent of my loneliness, he didn't stay with me every day.

I soon discovered that film-studios have a smell and atmosphere entirely different from anything else. The visitor steps into this fantasy the moment he passes the rigid security checks on the front gates. I developed a love-hate relationship for all this. At times I loved the sombre bustle of films being made, yet some times I loathed the artificiality of it when I had to grapple with effects of my quota, remember words, positions, names and directions, sweat under the hot arc-lights and make-up, shiver in the autumn rain as I ran to the studio bar, or just act.

There was one very interesting highlight of this otherwise miserable period. That was when I was asked to appear before the Government Committee on Youth. This was a body set up to look into the activities of young people. Like most government committees, it was created a long time after any problem had existed.

Teenagers as such had died out then, young adults between fifteen and twenty-one were being accepted as free-thinking individuals with the right to be discerning in all they did and with the money they spent. People had become used to their promiscuity and no longer regarded it as a shocking subject one didn't discuss.

I lammed into that committee with a vehemence they didn't anticipate. Sensibly, the meeting had been set early in the morning so I wasn't high at the time. I had, however, had a swig at the rum-bottle, purely for medicinal purposes of course. The remarks I made, they said, would be in confidence. I believed them and this gave me a chance to let rip.

They wanted me to talk as a teenager first and a pop singer second. Why they thought I would be articulate on young people, I don't know. I suspect now that there must have been a shrewd publicity man on the Government's behalf at work here. They wanted to give their little committee a boost, and this was the way, interviewing the nation's teenage hero, Danny Gabriel.

After the interview, which lasted three hours and utterly finished me, I came out to meet the press. I was dead beat, but fortunately John was around with a thermos flask of hot rum and Oxo. I sank in one of those deep club armchairs, looking a weak figure surrounded by those gargantuan pressmen, most of whom knew me of old and could almost write this interview without bothering to leave their offices.

I was bound to give the same old answers. They asked standard questions at first about youth clubs, pop music, hooliganism and the interview seemed pretty flat. Then a new man whom I hadn't seen before, asked the sixty-four thousand dollar question.

"I suppose you didn't have much to tell them about sex, did you Danny?"

Up to then, I was my usual meek country boy image. But I was weary and irritable after a morning of talking.

"What makes you think that?" I snapped back. There was a rustle of notebooks.

"Well it's not what people associate with you, is it —I mean your guitar is supposed to be your only love. What could you tell this committee about teenagers and sex?"

"A damn sight more than you could," I shouted. The cameras crackled. "Look—just because I look like a bleeding angel when I'm on stage, it doesn't mean I am off it. I've had more sex in the past three weeks than I reckon you've had in your life, whack, even leaving out the orgies." I could almost hear the pressmen scribbling furiously.

"I gave that committee all I could. Kids are lonely, desperately lonely. They are also a healthy randy lot and I don't reckon they should be suppressed. Sex isn't dirty, you know, it's beautiful. And it's thanks to people like the press who always mention sex as filthy instead of something private, that kids get so mixed up when they find themselves reacting in a normal healthy way."

I was aware of John stepping in front of me, frantically trying to stop the interview before any more damage was done.

"I don't know much about love, except it's a heartbreaker. But with sex—straightforward lust—you know where you are. There's no hurdy-gurdy emotion business there. I've been in love, but it hasn't worked out. I'm still lonely. Sex is the thing for me, and lots of it."

That night Bernard and myself decided by mutual agreement not to renew my contract with him when it came up for review on my birthday in January.

CHAPTER 16

It's all moving up to the present now. The shudders are going, there's only the flat feeling of remorse as I look back. There was that time I woke up in Lucy's bed with a long scratch down my cheek, and a thick black scab forming. I had come to her weeping about four that morning, blind drunk. She didn't know who had scratched me and neither did I. There was just a feeling of deep regret, as though I had violated someone I liked and would never have touched if I'd been sober. Even now I don't know what happened, but still have a knot of horror in my stomach at the things I've done but can't recall.

There were more and more days like that after my break with Bernard. Filming took up a lot of time until Christmas. I struggled through somehow spending most of my time at the studio bar then frantically being dabbed with powder to make me look the healthy country-boy I was supposed to be. I was in a flexible daze most of the time, doing exactly what I was told then shuffling back to the nearest bottle.

Bernard was still my manager until 23rd January. But he explained that it would be embarrassing for him to get me bookings now, especially as he had other commitments to fill in that field. I met these other commitments briefly when I called at Bernard's flat with John to collect my clothes. His name was Toby Jug, a tall gangling singer with a soft fleshy face and meek eyes: Bernard's new dagger with which to attack stardom. I was really out.

Living somewhere was a problem. I had got so used to living out of a suitcase that for a while I just tried to assimilate touring by toting my bag from flat to flat staying with friends of various sexes. After a couple of days, I got bored and moved on. John, who had agreed to take over managing me, was trying to tie up arrangements with Debroy Martin, my agent. The agents themselves were doubtful about my career, especially as my Christmas record (Bernard's choice) had flopped so dismally. It was unfortunate in being called

"Holy Virgin" - considering what I told the press about my views on love and sex.

My agents were waiting for a showcase that would properly gauge public opinion. TV and radio were cautious about me. Normally, an outburst like mine to the press wouldn't have mattered if it had come from a more sophisticated singer. But it was in such contrast to my public image that I had to suffer for it. Fans, promoters, everyone, were confused.

Curiously, this blank period around Christmas time, didn't lead me to drinking very much more. This was due to two reasons. The first was that, kipping uncertainly where I could, had made me think that what I really needed to stabilize me was a place of my own. For a time I toyed with the idea of buying a farm but remembering how hopeless I was with the administration side of farming and that my own talent was on the sheer labouring side, there didn't seem much point.

I wasn't contemplating leaving the business then, and saw no reason why I should burden myself unnecessarily. So then my ideal changed to a house. I started stomping the countryside, by myself, although I much preferred to take a bird along with me whenever I could find one, to view various properties throughout the home counties.

One Sunday I got up early and drove down to a village near Slough. I knew that the house I was going to look at would be too far away from London, but I went nevertheless. And this is the second reason for taking a slight grip of myself. My search.

I had begun searching, unconsciously at first, for a far more stabilizing influence than a house. I had been brought up in the strict conventions of a church-attending community. I couldn't remember the last time I had been to church but, when I saw the spire of the very English church in that village, I hoped I would find the answer to my search inside.

The church itself had trappings about it which brought memories of Thickley flooding back to my mind. To enter it, the congregation had to walk through a farm which surrounded the church. On either side where shippons and barns and a defiant Aberdeen Angus bull stalking around his pen. There were pigs, and hens scurrying around. The smells of dung and cattle cake, and the noise of animals fidgeting to be out in the fields, set me in a solemn mood as I walked through into the church.

Since it was Sunday, there were a lot of people there. I sat near the back, in the shadow of a pillar cast on the pew as light filtered through a Technicolour window. Judging by the congregation, I guessed that this was a phoney sort of village. There were more city types there than country-people. Unfortunately, I got to the church before the service started and, although I tried to look inconspicuous, most people noticed the blond sad-eyed stranger they had got in their midst.

Before long I could hear whispers behind tattered hymn books and saw heads turning to admire the font which had been there for generations, just to check if I really was Danny Gabriel. I tried to ignore it, giving myself to the service. That first hymn had a strange effect on me; it was as though here I had really found home; the same feeling I had had three years before in that Liverpool coffee bar!

I was jerked back to unpleasant reality during the waffling sermon when the vicar made reference to "the famous visitor we have with us, who despite his fame, has come to worship with us and humble himself in front of God."

I wanted that hard old pew to crack right open and turn into my coffin. Heads bobbing round like fairground Aunt Sallys glanced at me mockingly. I could see people straining at the leash held by the vicar, desperate for the service to end so that they could get at me. Most people showed the signs of thinking either "he's come-here-for-publicity" or "why-doesn't-he-take-his-big-time-attitude away -from -our-lovely-little -church -and-go -back -where-he belongs". I wanted to die.

The service came to an end, and I nipped smartly down the aisle to the door. It was just my luck that an over-eager teenager and her imposing mum got there before me.

And it honestly wasn't my fault that an astute cameraman happened to be waiting outside the church for a Christening couple. There was the tip-off...the photograph: and Danny Gabriel coming out of church surrounded by admiring fans. A quick quote from a mum: "Any boy who can find the time to go to church when he is so famous is the sort of boy I'd like my daughter to marry," and the press had got a story.

I ran through the farmyard and jumped into the Rover. I was terrified. On the way home back to London, I stopped the car. I was physically and violently sick on the grass verge as I contemplated the outcome of my "Search." In the eyes of God where it meant nothing, my fame had snared me. I wasn't worried about the publicity - which would make me a laughing stock after what I'd told the press - it was as though I'd suddenly discovered that my parents weren't really mine at all.

The following Sunday, 22nd December, I decided to try again. It wasn't that I was essentially a religious person, nor felt that deeply about God. I suppose I was just trying to lose myself in a safe atmosphere similar to the one I had known at Thickley.

I remember polishing off half a bottle of Blue-Nun with a boiled egg for breakfast. I was staying at the flat of a young aristocrat. He was a wealthy debs-escort type without much interest in me. He had given me a key to his flat and I used it and his spare bedroom whenever I wanted to. The arrangement suited us perfectly. He would sometimes mention to his friends about the amusing pop singer he had staying with him, but at the same time never pestered me with those friends.

I decided this time to try a different kind of church. What made me choose Quakers I don't know, but they had always seemed more natural and free-thinking than other religions. I remember once seeing the Meeting House in Chester and asking mum what people did there. She had told me that Quakers were very good people; were a sensible religion but didn't like singing or dancing.

So it was with some trepidation that I pulled up outside

a hall proclaiming Friends' Meeting House, a few miles out of London. In a way, I suppose I wanted to challenge these people to turn me away.

Pushing open the door I found I was in a small hall with a very high roof with beams stretched across it. The most striking feature of the building was the polished wood floor. Someone had obviously spent hours on it. A large and welcoming coal fire warmed the room and round it, set out like a debating chamber, were rows of chairs. At the back of the hall were even armchairs.

About thirty people were in the room, and were settling themselves down. I sunk into one of the armchairs aware that I must have looked very much a stranger. One or two people glanced at me, nodded courteously, then busied themselves with their own thoughts. At eleven o'clock, silence embraced the hall.

During the next hour I rediscovered peace. I had never before sat in a room full of people in complete silence, utterly alone, and yet been so much part of the meeting. I found a tranquillity in that hall (just off a thundering trunk road to London) which I didn't know existed.

There were no religious motifs and models and no snob-value churchgoers. Yet there was more of God there that I had known before. For the first twenty minutes, it was a strain for me to accustom myself to the wall of silence. Then as my thoughts flowed, I discovered it wasn't a wall but more a cradled arm helping me along.

About three people got up and spoke. They did this casually, without any show of having thought about it. They talked about everyday things, but in such a way as to make them seem more beautiful. One lady, in a green hat and wobble-spectacles, even read a letter from a friend in Canada. It was all tremendously moving.

I found I was hanging on to their words, letting the idea they generated take over my mind. I could almost feel something building-up inside me which could urge me to leap to my feet and add to the general thought process of the meeting. Promptly at noon, without any guidance from anyone, the silence left us, feet shuffled, and people who had seemed relaxed before, looked warm and fortified.

For the next few weeks, I looked into Quaker beliefs. I found I was very much mistaken about a lot of things. I even found that my drinking didn't exclude me, so long as I didn't corrupt other people. The publication of their pamphlet on sex which I read before I made my debut at the meeting, proved to me that I had chosen the most enlightened religion in Britain.

The only snag to me really achieving the object of my search was that that I couldn't accept the biblical teaching. My days with moralizing musicians had created a whole set of doubts. In the end, I sublimated my search in the campaign to buy a home.

Eventually I found the nobly named "Grange" in Northwood. It was a huge house with a few acres of ground set just beyond a wood and with a view of the last remaining acres of farm land in Middlesex.

I know that a little thatched cottage in Sussex would have done me just as well, but I had the impression that the bigger my home, the more stable I would be. In preparation for all kinds of wild house parties, I changed one of the rooms into a kind of gymnasium with wall bars and a table-tennis table. I made another room the billiards-lounge, with a huge table and all the necessary equipment. I also put fruit machines in there, a little bar, some card tables and juke box.

My lounge was the height of luxury, with the most expensive and elaborate high-fi equipment to blend with the furniture. My own taste wasn't very good, so I brought in a professional interior decorator to style everything.

All the bedrooms, there were seven, had TV and a gramophone. The grounds, attended by a regular gardener, were mostly picturesque gardens, although there was a fair-sized paddock where I could graze a horse, as soon as I bought one.

To run a house like that called for some staff. I fancied having a resident housekeeper until I decided that an older woman might not approve of all that I hoped would go on in the house. Instead, I engaged a woman to come in each day, but live out. For my own needs, and as a professional companion, I engaged a valet.

I was all set, when I eventually moved in during February, for a life time of orgies and drinking in my dream home. It was after my sensational house-warming which lasted four days and ended with an unscheduled, but spectacular, suicide by a starlet cutting her wrists in my swimming pool, that I began to discover the loneliness of my home.

I appreciated being able to walk in the woods, and stroll along the paths of my garden just contemplating the beauty of the scenery, but I was twenty-two now, not the carefree lad who was once as much part of the countryside as a newborn lamb.

Inside the house I was desperately lonely. I was so used to having people around me, and had catered for them in the house, that without them I was just lost. Lucy stayed there occasionally and other girls from time to time. So did a few friends and I welcomed them—but there was no one regularly.

When I was working, things weren't so bad. John had done a deal with another agency and I was booked on package-shows featuring a new singer as the star. Now I was just one of the many has-been strewn about the pop world. The type who haven't got the sense to get out while they're on top but frantically cling, hoping their next record will shoot them back again. Even now, my next record still hasn't been released, which shows how bad things are.

A typical day when I wasn't working began with me breakfasting either in bed or in the kitchen on an egg and, according to my hangover, Fernet Branca or Champagne. I decided that having earned my money I was going to spend it. I found that champagne put me in an excellent frame of mind for the day. I then pretended to work, either with the guitar or pounding the piano I had installed in the music room. This didn't last long.

Sometimes I dragged the valet out for a game of table tennis and at eleven, I drove down to the pub about a mile away for a drink before lunch. I left at closing time, and then—according to my mood—went home or to the drinking club in Bushey, where I had played three years previously. If that happened, I was knackered for the day. If I did get home in the afternoon, then I'd laze around until the pubs opened again in the evening.

I was going berserk with all this drinking. In a pub, I often got the feeling that everyone was watching me. I used to twist my head nervously all the time trying to catch people out. I had to drink faster so that I wouldn't mind if they were watching. And sometimes I'd think I was swallowing my tongue. I was choking, I was going to die. I had to have some quick doubles to relax me.

Often I could have sworn people were following me. I ran from pub to pub trying to escape them, taking my drink to the gents, knocking it back, then scrambling out of the window. Rarely did I know a sober minute.

Yet, always when I woke up in the morning, I'd be at home in my own bed. Sometimes there was a girl with me, other times I'd still have my clothes on. I used to come home by taxi, and the valet would spend a lot of the next day trying to trace my car.

In my alcoholic daze my world was one of complete fantasy. There was drink, girls—there would always be girls—and my guitar. That was all. Providing people made sure that I got all three nothing could go wrong. Miraculously I managed a two-week tour round the country without being too obstreperous.

I had John and another man as chauffeur-cum-bandsman constantly with me. John tried to regulate my drinking, but it was no use. I had so much alcohol in my blood that even if I only drank water for two days I would still be drunk. John just dressed me, stuck the guitar in my hand, pushed me on stage and prayed. I knew what to do in front of the footlights, and I still had an army of fans. They screamed and cheered for me, and I played up to them. A right nit I must have looked.

The inevitable crisis came a few weeks ago. I had been

booked in a show at a cinema fairly near Northwood. John had pleaded with the valet and chauffeur to keep their eyes on me that day, as he knew that—on my own stamping ground—I'd probably have more to drink than usual. I started the day bright and early with champagne, and then got on to gin and cider during the morning. After lunch I persuaded the chauffeur to take me to my drinking-club, just for a few drinks before we went to the cinema.

Now, I was well used to getting away from imaginary people who were following me, so it was a simple matter giving the chauffeur the slip. Admittedly, there wasn't anywhere to go as all the pubs were closed. But I had acquired a bottle of brandy, which I took to the cinema and hid in my dressing room for later. Unfortunately, I got the impression that the building was about to collapse, so I had to have a few swigs to make me feel a bit happier about it.

The time came for the show and John, knowing I hadn't been outside the theatre since opening time, and also having searched my guitar case and wardrobe-bag for booze, thought I was all right. But when I was left alone in the room, I rummaged through the waste bin, hauled out my hidden brandy, took long raw draughts, then tried to look as sweet as I did before.

I got through most of the bottle waiting for my turn to go on stage. I honestly didn't know what I was doing and have only pieced this together from what I've heard since.

John pointed me in the right direction and pushed me on stage. The kids screamed and I was having a ball. But suddenly, in the middle of "Let Me Go" I wanted a piss. Quite calmly, I walked over to the proscenium arch, unzipped my fly and proceeded to urinate over the audience.

CHAPTER 17

This is a pleasant hospital. They are letting me use the telephone now. Mary says I am over the worst, and they don't drug me so much. I spend most of the day propped up on a comfortable mound of pillows. They make me wear pyjamas, and they feel warm and friendly; I haven't worn pyjamas since Thickley. I feel clean, almost normal; almost well.

I think I'll play that guitar soon.

It is tea-time now, and any minute I expect Mary to stride in with my cup of tea, three paste sandwiches and a cake on a tray. I shall eat the food and then take a green and yellow plastic bomb they have prescribed for me after every meal. Those are the sedatives, I think.

The other tablets, my red ones, are my "buse'" tablets. That's my private word for booze. They are anti-drink. The very thought of a drink now makes me feel sick. The doctor says that when I leave here, I won't want to touch a drink, ever. It will just make me sick. Every day he offers me one, and I don't fancy it!

Sometimes I phone people and chat to them. To help pass the afternoon, I like a few friends to drop in. That boy Dave from Brighton was here the other day. We had a long chat and, when I come out, he is going to take me to the Brighton Meeting House which he says I'll like. A lot of birds phone me up, including one I'm sure I don't know but who says she's desperate for me to come round and see her new flat and how she's got this big four poster-bed with black leather sheets. My mum rings up, too, and she wants me to go down there for a rest when I come out.

I'll probably be discharged in a few days. It's all up to me really. I don't know if drink will still be a problem when I get out. Compared with other pop stars, I seem to have taken a fair beating. Of course, a lot of stars' failings never reach the public eye. Those who drink like me are occasionally whisked away suffering from nervous exhaustion and then emerge as though nothing has happened and without a single lost fan.

Others like myself have our disgraces made public. Sins often overtake a pop singer and I don't think I'm very exceptional in my own way of life. All of them without exception charver like mad, although one or two might be a bit kinky.

Looking back, it's easy for me to find people and incidents to blame for my own failure. Maybe my managers did run me too hard, like a machine and ignoring my own personality. Although I became an alcoholic and a randy sod, underneath perhaps Mary is right and I am still the nice guy I was before.

It's just that Bernard and his colleagues chose an image for me which was really too hard to live up to. That seemed to give them the right to boss my personal life as well. I was so much a cherry-boy at heart, all peasant-like and virginal, that it was easy for me to let them.

I guess I drank because I thought it gave me the colour I was lacking through being so inexperienced. When I was told that my heart had weakened, I was really chuffed. To me that meant, well, maybe I wasn't so perfect as the press said.

I failed through success. Success is judged by the public as how many times one's name appears in the papers, taking pretty girls to first nights, waving good bye at airports, signing autographs, record-shattering fees and all that. This is the phoney part of success and it tends to obscure the real part of it - honest technical accomplishment. I was mixed up separating the flattery from sincere comment.

As my own "success" depended more on the impact of my mythical-image rather than my singing and my guitar playing ability, I didn't stand much chance of sorting things out sensibly. This had odd effects on some people. Aunts and Uncles—people who had known me since I was a baby—clamoured for my autograph. I discovered I'd got cousins who would never have bothered with me otherwise. There were suddenly thousands of people who seemed to be related to someone in Thickley and regarded this as a right to invade my most intimate moments.

If I had the chance again, I think I would still take it. I

loved playing the guitar and singing, and in spite of the per-ilous position I am in now, I don't think I have any regrets, even though I've slipped from the big time.

The world hasn't ended for me just yet although it is pret-ty near it. I don't know what I will do when I leave here. This pop side of show business is a drug far more demanding than pep pills or brandy. One moment I want to get out for good, the next moment I don't. If I did give up the business, I've got nowhere else to go.

If I stay, I know I'll never be more than a has-been, how-ever much better I might perform through being sober. I'll be on the professional fringe again, traipsing around the country in a beat-up van with a third-rate group trying to recapture some of my former glory. But I'd still be playing my guitar whatever the motives.

In actual fact, I've got to do something fairly quickly. The house and my drinking have set me back quite considerably and in fact I'm dead broke. Not much of the house belongs to me either. If I sold it I'd get about five thousand pounds for myself- nothing to moan at for a farm-labourer, but a meagre pension for a pop-singer.

I just don't know what to do - stay in the business where I haven't got a hope and try once again to grapple with all the dangers attendant to it - or sell up, clear out and, taking my guitar, go abroad singing and playing to my heart's delight.

I wonder where my passport is?

POSTSCRIPT

The following, written in ballpoint in his unmistakable childish scrawl, is the final entry in Danny Gabriel's diary:

"Adam Cole, producer "Happy Heidi" visited with John... says film sneak preview great success...me sensational! ... Theme song—the one I cut November?—just released and climbing to Number One! I'm booked for personal appearances to boost film and it's to have a Royal Premier... he's got me the lead part in a Hollywood movie in a kind of James Dean role... John says he's lining up an Australian tour too...

"So the big time rolls on...this time I'm ready for it!"